New Ghost Stories III

New Ghost Stories III
The Fiction Desk Anthology Series
Volume Eleven

Edited by Rob Redman

The Fiction Desk

First published in 2017 by The Fiction Desk Ltd.

ISBN 978-0-9927547-7-8

The stories contained within this volume are works of fiction. Any
resemblence between people or businesses depicted in these stories
and those existing in the real world is entirely coincidental.

Please see our website for current contact
details and submissions information.

www.thefictiondesk.com

Printed and bound in the UK by Imprint Digital.

Contents

Introduction

Rob Redman

What is it about the supernatural that has led us to publish three volumes of ghost stories? Our anthologies are generally mixed collections: we don't publish dedicated volumes of other genres, although their stories might appear from time to time in our pages. How then have ghost stories come to receive this special treatment?

As with many of life's questions, the answer can be found in a good bottle of Scotch.

Whisky lovers will often add two or three drops of water to their drink. This creates an exothermic reaction that raises the temperature of the liquid slightly and helps to release various aromas and flavours, changing the nature of the whisky. Tasting notes for a bottle will sometimes promise two quite distinct experiences, before and after the addition of water. In fiction, and perhaps especially in short fiction with its concentrated focus (what you might call its cask-strength nature), a drop of the supernatural can achieve the same thing, opening out the themes and revealing new aspects and ideas in the story.

As you go back in the history of the printed short story, closer to its origins in collected oral traditions and folk tales, the division between so-called realistic fiction and ghost stories all but disappears, and the supernatural becomes a normal aspect of storytelling. There are just stories, which sometimes feature ghosts, depending on whether or not the writer has chosen to add those drops of water to their tale.

In this volume are seven of those stories – the ones that happen to feature ghosts, or something like them. These include the winners of our last two ghost story competitions: Will Dunn and Barney Walsh took first prizes, Philippa East and Jerry Ibbotson were second, and Seth Marlin and Richard Agemo third.

The history of short stories does not lack narrators who want to order up a drink and tell you their tale, but in this case, it pays to take a glass of your own and listen closely. After all, this is a man who knows a bit about obsession, sacrifice, and the lengths to which people will go in pursuit of their goals.

Des Nuits Blanches

Will Dunn

You shouldn't believe a word of what I'm about to tell you, okay? Not a word. *Pourqoui? Parce que je suis... pardon...* For one thing, I am drunk. Speaking of which, *Téri!, encore un p'tit verre...* and for another thing, I am old. And we have only just met. But you like *les velos*, you said, and I told you, it used to be my work: le Tour de France.

No, ha ha, not on the bike. Do I look like an athlete to you? No, I worked on *les journaux*, the papers. I haven't written anything for a long time now. How long? The last time I covered a race was in 1970, that's how long. A hot afternoon, very hot, and then on the mountain it was cold. We weren't dressed for it; we crowded together like penguins. And then we heard it: the roar of the crowd, moving up the road beneath us like a living thing, and we knew he was coming. The champion, Eddy Merckx, half a kilometre from the finish and over a minute ahead. A minute is a long time on

Mont Ventoux. As he passed us I saw his right hand go up, as if he was going to wave, but he did not. Instead he took off his cap, and with it he made the sign of the cross.

But you know about Eddy. Everyone knows about him. The *maillot jaune*, the green, the mountains, the Paris-Roubaix. He won the Giro d'Italia too, five times. He made the normal riders into a joke, he just broke away and left them to fight for second place. Everyone said he was making history, that there had never been anyone like him. But me, I was an old fart even then. I was finished with the mountains. And I had seen riding like that before.

When I first began covering the races, I wasn't a writer. I was a photographer. I got the job when I was sixteen years old, because I was very thin. Yes! I know, I don't look it now, but when I was a boy, I was light as a bird. They needed someone skinny, very light, to go on the back of a motorbike and take pictures. You can't have some big fat bastard on a bike like that: you'll crash, you won't get up the mountains. And of course I wanted to, I would have done it for free. Ten years I spent, holding on to the back of a motorbike with just my thighs, camera in both hands, and through the lens I saw Coppi and Anquetil and Bobet. I make new prints from those films, sometimes. You can always improve them with a good print.

Some pictures I look at more often, these days. I'm getting very old now, and the winters here are unpredictable.

There is one I've been looking at lately, of a young rider climbing a very steep Alpine road, standing on the pedals and hauling away on the handlebars, holding the drops like a sprinter, using his upper body to force his bike into the slope. An interesting riding position, for sure. But the main thing about this photograph is his face.

There's an expression many cyclists get when they're exhausted, when they're in agony. Their skin goes pale and thin, their eyes dart around as they try to focus, their mouths hang kind of loose, so you can see their bottom row of teeth. But the rider in the picture does not look like that. His face is set, his eyes are fixed. He looks more as if he is afraid.

He was from the Haute-Loire. His name was Sylvain T—. You wouldn't have heard of him. He won a few stages; mountain stages, in the smaller tours, and he did well in the Basque tour. An excellent climber, but always a domestique. A team rider: it was his job to put someone else on the finish line.

This picture I'm talking about, it was on the Tourmalet, in 1958. He won by two minutes. I have another of him on a climb in the Picos de Europa, in '57. I was behind Sylvain this time, but he was looking over his shoulder. Again, he was climbing on his own, forcing his way up a... you would call it now a 'first-category climb'; in my day we called it a big fat bitch of a hill. In that picture, he isn't looking at me — at the camera — but past me, down the road behind us. Again, he was winning by a long way. The peloton was half a mile behind him, he wouldn't have been able to see them. But his face, his expression. I never saw a face like that, not in a cycling photograph.

He was my friend.

A photographer has to know as much about the peloton as a writer. You've got to know whose picture to take, and from the first time I saw him race — he didn't win, but I knew Sylvain was good. Some riders in those days, they hated to be buzzed by a motorbike, they shouted at us. But Sylvain didn't care. He liked it. We got to know each other pretty well. At the end of the season one year, I told him I was going back to Italy; we lived in Breno, then, my wife is from there. He cycled there from Lyon, just arrived one day on his bike with a couple of panniers on the back, and we said of course, stay as long as you like. And we meant it, you know. Everyone liked Sylvain.

I suppose you would call it an accident, what happened, or an episode.

He stayed with us for a few nights, we sat around the kitchen table, myself and my wife and Sylvain and a couple of our friends from the village, and we ate and drank, long hours, and Sylvain would tell all these stories about the Tours he rode. I had some stories of my own, but they weren't as good. And then he asked if he could stay a little longer, to train in the high mountains.

I remember the first night he went out. It was dark and cold outside, and Sylvain appeared at the front door with his bike and his gloves and a scarf around his face. He said to me, I'm going to do my training now, I'll be back in a few hours.

'Now?' I said. 'You're going cycling now? Why?'

And he told me it was good to train at night. He said going out into the mountains, it was peaceful and empty and still, and on a clear night, which it was, you could cycle by moonlight. He said it's what he did back in France, he said he spent whole nights out on the mountain roads, alone, in the cold autumn nights before the snows came in and he had to go south and cycle during the day like everyone else.

Of course, we lived in a little mountain village, and everyone knew we had this funny French guy from my job — which, by the way, was thought a little glamorous in those days — staying at our house, so it didn't take long for people to hear about him cycling at night. They all thought it was pretty funny. Only one person, my wife's mother, didn't think it was funny. She was with us one day for lunch; Sylvain was telling us how far he'd climbed the previous night, way up into the peaks, and I saw she was getting agitated. She was a very quiet lady, she didn't talk much, but she raised her voice and said, 'You shouldn't go up to those places at night, Sylvain. It's not the same, on our side of the mountains. It's dangerous here at night.'

He was a gentleman. He nodded, and he agreed, but he said it was his duty to put himself in danger. For the race, he said.

But he also said that he would take it easy. Because when he rode into the night, and he was tired and he had no more sugar left in his blood, he started to see strange things – shapes, moving between the trees, that disappeared when he looked at them. And once, he said, he thought he saw a figure, a white figure sort of beckoning him towards the forest.

'That's when you know you need to eat, or you'll slow down, or pass out,' he said, and my wife smiled and got him another plate of pasta. But her mother looked at him like he was crazy.

Winter began to draw closer then, and as the sun was setting one day Sylvain said he was going out for a few hours. He'd be back before it got too late, he said, now that it was getting cold. Well, we had our dinner and we kept a plate warm by the stove. It must have been five, six hours, my wife had gone to bed a long time before. I fell asleep reading by the stove. And suddenly I was awoken by this noise, this thud, and then this gasping, rattling sound. It was Sylvain. He was scrabbling at the door, trying to get it open, but his hands were frozen, he was gasping for breath. I opened the door and he almost fell in, and when I helped him to a chair I felt that he was shaking.

I put his bike round the side of the house and I remember touching one of the tyres. It was cold, a clear night; there would have been patches of ice on some of the mountain roads by morning. But his tyres were warm. He must have really flown down that last descent, I thought. And in the dark, too.

I gave him some brandy and he told me he'd been chased by wolves. I didn't believe him but he could hardly talk, he was so exhausted. He slept all that night and the next day until early evening. I took him a plate of pasta, then another one, and then we had a glass of wine and he started to talk about the previous night.

He said he knew it wouldn't be long before the snows set in, and once that happened, he wouldn't be able to train like this any more until the spring. So he had gone looking for a serious climb, high in the mountain passes. Two, three hours he went up through the twisting backroads, never once seeing another person or even a passing car. It was a big full autumn moon, and it was a clear night, so he hardly needed the little light we'd made him put on the front of his bike. The road gleamed, he said, and it was so dark in the valleys that it seemed to him that he was riding along a bridge of silver that led high, high up into the night sky. When he felt like he was at the apex of his ride, he stopped, took his bearings, and headed back; but at some point he took a wrong turn. Each road junction he came to seemed less familiar. He wasn't sure which road he was on, he wasn't even sure which mountain. But he said to himself, it's fine — just descend, find a town, and there will be a signpost. So he pressed on, heading in what he thought was about the right direction.

Sylvain had told me before about previous rides, late at night and high up in the mountains, when he'd seen weird things at the edges of his vision. This is not so unusual for a cyclist: the legs run out of fuel, the brain is starved of sugar. As a professional, Sylvain knew to expect it. It was a symptom of how far he was pushing himself. All the same, he was captivated by how real it seemed. He would see something moving between the trees, he said, and sometimes a figure that seemed to be waving, or beckoning, but when he turned his head from the road there was of course nothing there.

On this night, however, it was different. It was no fleeting image that he saw. It was standing in the middle of the road.

He saw it from a long way off, as he came around a bend in the road that skirted the edge of the mountain. As he rounded the corner he could see along the sweep of road that bent downwards and into the curve of the hill, and in the belly of the curve was what he thought was a person. From his point of view it seemed almost like the silhouette of a woman, he said, all in white, with a dress billowing out at the base and a slender body on top. She was facing away from him, staring at the peak just above. He stopped pedalling, but he did not stop moving; his momentum carried him silently forward.

As he approached, he realised that he was further away from it than he had thought. It could not be a woman; it was taller than the pine trees that lined the edge of the road.

Soon he was within a hundred metres, and still he was trying to make sense of what he saw. As the road banked down towards the billowing white shape, he pulled on his brakes for the first time. The cold rubber brake blocks gave a screech, and the figure in the road turned to look at him.

It was hard for Sylvain to describe. It looked at him with eyes, he said, and he was sure it had teeth, and limbs, but he couldn't say how many of any of those things it had. Its form didn't make sense to him. It changed shape. It reared up for a moment, surprised, then hunkered very quickly and smoothly against the road, like a cat setting its shoulders towards its prey. It made no noise whatsoever.

Sylvain was not a superstitious man, much less a coward. In his rational mind he still thought he was seeing things. But his instincts told him what to do. He could feel the malevolence and hunger of the thing in the road. He could smell it. He turned around and began to pedal, hard, looking back through the crook of his left arm at the road behind. It began to move after him. He pedalled faster, and it started to move more urgently.

He was a good descender, Sylvain, and he took every downward turn faster than he would dare, even in a race, but it stayed with him. Even on the long, steep straights, when he locked his elbows against his chest and plunged into the valley at a hundred, a hundred and ten kilometres an hour. His eyes filled with water and he prayed that the roaring he heard was only the wind in his ears. When he looked back, he couldn't tell if it was running or floating, billowing down the road behind him like a cloud with eyes and claws. Again he looked back and it seemed solid, like a great predatory animal. Twice he had to go into climbs, and he threw himself into them like they were sprints, hauling away on the bars for ten, twenty minutes at a time, throwing himself up the mountain away from that terrible white demon. It took him two hours to find his way back to our village, and it chased him the whole way.

I didn't know what to believe. Of course, I told him he could not ride in darkness any more. It was too cold in the mountains now, and a crash at night could easily be fatal. He agreed, and he seemed relieved to have spoken of it. He would spend a couple more days with us, then return to France.

Then, on the morning he was due to leave, I found him looking at the big map of our region that we used to have on the wall in the kitchen there. He showed me the descent he thought he'd taken to get back into town that night. I told him he was still lost. To get around to that pass, he would had to have covered three more mountains, big ones, in a couple of hours. The whole trip would have been over two hundred kilometres.

'By God,' he said, 'If a hallucination can make me ride like that, maybe it is a pity I don't have more hallucinations.'

This is what makes someone a true racing cyclist, I think. He will do anything to improve himself. He will find the most appalling thing in the world and embrace it, if he thinks it will make him a champion. At that time, I did not realise this was true of Sylvain T—.

I did not see him again until the next season began. Sylvain entered some single races, and I saw in the papers that he did very well, but it was in the mountains that he excelled. There was a race near Grenoble — they don't run it now, but it was a big event back then. Most of the serious contenders for the *maillot jaune* in the Tour would ride also in Grenoble, to take a look at the rest of the field.

There were five climbs. For three of them, there wasn't much to talk about. A group of four, five riders got away — two, three minutes ahead — but we were pretty sure they would be caught. Sylvain was in the middle of the peloton; it looked like it was going to be an unremarkable race for him. I was on the motorbike, concentrating on the small group of riders who were a few minutes ahead, when he passed us. I was happy when I saw him. I thought he was going to join the front group, work with them, maybe help them stay ahead of the race. That's what any rider in his right mind would have done. But he carried on past them, on his own. They laughed at him, of course. He would never stay ahead, there were still two mountains to go. I shouted something to him, I forget what — some warning, or encouragement. But then we got ahead of him for a photo, I could see in his face that he couldn't hear me. He had that look, that mask on his face. The white mask of terror.

He won by six minutes. I still have my last two pictures from that day: one of Sylvain crossing the finish line, his face drawn and exhausted. He just about managed to get his arms in the air. But the next photo is remarkable. Most riders cross the line and roll past the crowd, they get themselves some food. If they've won by six minutes, they celebrate. But in my last picture from that race, Sylvain has stopped, just beyond the chequered boxes painted on the road. People are looking at him strangely, but he does not see them. He is staring back down the road, his hands on the grips. He looks as if he is ready to set off again.

I looked for him after that race, but he had already left. I didn't see him again until the Giro d'Italia began. It started early that year, and in the mountains it was still very cold.

I found him in his room after one of the early stages. He hadn't been doing well. His team didn't like him — he was a great rider but they thought he was selfish, or crazy — and on the flat stages he was just keeping up.

'Cheer up,' I told him. 'Soon we will be in the mountains.'

I do not need a photograph to remember the look he gave me. He was wrapped up in many layers of clothing, although it was not a cold night. He sat hunched on his bed, holding his knees. In that little hotel room, I thought he looked like a prisoner. I asked him what was wrong, although I suspected it already.

'It waits for me there,' he said. 'In the mountains.'

Then he told me, to my horror, what had happened after the incident that night in the peaks, when he had met something on the road that had chased him. He had been ready to go home, to rest and do his winter training as usual. He cycled out of our village and began heading for Bergamo, where he was supposed to get the train. But as he rode, he could not help thinking about how far he had ridden, how fast, when the terror was at his wheel.

He got as far as the next village, where he stopped at the *tabac* to buy some stamps, and saw there by chance a card advertising a small chalet up the mountain. It was cheap, and when he asked in the village he found it was still available.

And so he did not go home to France, as I thought he had, but stayed in the mountains. He went back up into the high passes at night, looking for his white demon to chase him, to make him fast, as it had that night. And he found it – or it found him. Somewhere up there, in the darkness, it picked up his scent again. The terror of that thing, boiling and whispering along the road behind him. The hunger it gave off. The endless, freezing malice. It made him ride like never before.

'Did you see it in Grenoble?' I asked, but I knew the answer. I had seen his face.

'It waits for me,' he repeated. 'It can find me, anywhere.'

As the race moved up into the mountains, Sylvain began to show his form. It was scarcely believable, how he rode. There was no strategy to it. The race would reach a certain point and suddenly he would be away, pedalling frantically. You could see the tendons standing out in his arms, and the tips of his fingers that emerged from his gloves were white where they gripped the bars. He climbed like he was sprinting on a track, and he descended like a madman. We only saw him in the distance on the descents; even the motorbikes couldn't stay on him.

He should have been happy, of course. He won two of the most challenging stages, he was leading the mountains classification, people were beginning to look at him differently. But Sylvain could only think about what he saw each time they reached the high roads: something white that raced between the trees. From the corner of his eye it took on different forms, strange and sometimes beautiful; but as it came closer to the road he could hear its teeth snapping, he could feel the ice in its breath. Then he would start to pedal like crazy. The truth was that he hardly cared if he won the stage. He was pedalling for his life.

I tried to persuade him that it wasn't real. I told him that nobody else could see it.

'I can smell it,' he said. 'Usually I smell it before I see it. It smells like rotting flowers.'

I didn't know what to say to that. In the days that followed I tried calling around to find a psychoanalyst, but you have to remember that this was a very long time ago, and I was just a young man with a camera.

By the time we reached the highest of the mountain stages, Sylvain was poised to win the mountains jersey. It was a stage that suited his style: long, steep climbs; frightening descents. But the weather reports were bad, and there was talk of changing the route.

There were five climbs, each of them a monster; and the two highest passes, the last ones, were lost completely in the cloud. Officials were coming back from the steepest climbs in their cars saying there was no point, they were sweeping snow off the road. Hail had fallen on the previous stage, stones the size of Muscat grapes that left the riders' backs covered with bruises.

But I suppose you know what professional cyclists are like. Nobody tells them it's too wet or too dangerous.

I spoke to Sylvain before the race began. I tried to be positive for him. He had all that winter training, I said, all that experience in the cold, high places. But he could barely look at me.

'It's too soon,' he told me, and his voice was very quiet. I asked him what he meant.

'It's here,' he said, and I am ashamed to say that although we were in a busy car park, in broad daylight, I was afraid. 'It's here,' he repeated, 'too soon. I can smell it already.'

I knew then what he was going to do. We were hardly out of the first village when he started looking over his shoulder, edging his way to the front of the peloton, and you could see his team shaking their heads. Halfway up the second climb, he set off away from the group. Two other teams stuck with him until the next climb. He led them the entire way, and then dropped them like they were amateurs. At some point he seemed to change. His position became hunched. He kicked away up the mountain, and no one could keep up. The two of us on the motorbike followed him.

After a few minutes I realised that this time, Sylvain wasn't looking back over his shoulder. He was staring dead ahead. Good, I thought: perhaps he's stopped this nonsense. He's concentrating on winning. But then we got in front of him for a photo, and I saw his face was grey. He seemed hardly to notice us. He looked, I thought, as if it already had him in its teeth.

But still he climbed, and still we puttered ahead of him. As we got onto the fourth climb we began to move through the cloud layer. The wind started to whip around us and the hailstones rattled off our helmets. Sylvain was in pain, of course, but he didn't slow down. If anything his pedalling became more frantic. He crested the fourth high pass and my driver shouted that the next one would be worse, much worse. He was right.

The final climb, I hardly took any pictures. I was too worried for Sylvain, too worried for myself. We were being blown all over the road by these curtains of rain and hail and of course I was facing backwards on the motorbike, holding on with my knees. Even if I could have seen to take a picture, I could hardly feel my hands. Sylvain began to slow down.

I thought then, perhaps this is it. Perhaps he'll give up and he'll see there's nothing terrible in the fog, and that'll put an end to this nonsense. But each time Sylvain slowed for a minute or two, he would suddenly stiffen, like he'd heard something. His head would dip to look under his armpit, like a track cyclist does when he looks behind for his opponent, and his legs would start spinning, faster than before.

He was riding hard like that when it happened; dancing on the pedals, as they say. We were somewhere near the peak of the fifth climb. One moment we were ahead of him, and then there was a huge gust of wind and hail. Everything went white. When we could see again we were all on the ground, the driver and the motorbike and me. Sylvain too was sprawled on the road, just down the slope from us.

I rushed down to him, but he was already getting back on his bike. I tried to shout over the wind, to tell him to stop, that none of the other riders would make it up the mountain anyway. He was frantic. The chain had slipped on his bike and he was pulling it back into place, scrabbling at the teeth of his gears. Then he got the chain back on and he turned to me, and his face was terrible to see.

'*Mes lanières!*'

He screamed it at me above the wind. His feet, he meant: he needed me to strap his feet back into the pedals. I did. I gave him a push, and I watched my friend pedal away into the fog.

We couldn't go any further on the motorbike. It wasn't starting, and after five minutes in the howling weather we took shelter beneath an outcrop of rock at the side of the road. It took an hour before a car came for us. No other riders attempted that climb: they had abandoned the race after the fourth mountain. At the finish line, down in the valley on the other side of the mountain, they waited for three hours. Sylvain never appeared.

The race was postponed for two days. In those days there were only a few journalists, no TV. A story like this only went so far, if the race committee decided it wasn't good for business. The police carried on searching the gorges, but the race moved on.

I had sprained my wrist falling off the motorbike, so I asked my editor if I could be replaced. He wasn't happy but he understood, he knew Sylvain was a friend. I drove home. I waited to hear about Sylvain and I heard nothing.

The Giro finished a week later. I went to shoot the award ceremony, and afterwards I found the race doctor. We had a drink together, in his office, and we talked about Sylvain. I told him — perhaps not in so much detail as tonight, but I told him Sylvain's story.

I remember the doctor reaching into the metal filing cabinet by his desk and passing me an envelope. A big brown envelope, thick card, and inside were two little silver packets, like rolls of coins or sweets.

'Amphetamine,' said the doctor. 'A lot of the riders use it. Gives you energy, but it's not real energy. Very bad for the nerves, for the heart. Here is your white demon.'

Perhaps, I thought, that was it. I went back home, and still no news arrived about Sylvain. Still he was missing. A week, two weeks later, I unpacked my cameras.

I knew, of course, that there was a roll of film still in my camera from the last race. I didn't want to develop it, but I knew I would have to one day. Better to get it over with, I thought.

The darkroom in my house is only big enough for one person to stand up, but it's all I need. Once I processed the film, I started to make some prints. I didn't make contact sheets in those days — paper was too expensive — so I just viewed them in the enlarger, one by one.

In some of the pictures, I remember, he had a brave smile. In others, he seemed not to notice the camera at all. Finally I got to the last few images, and it looked as if my camera had been damaged by the fall, like the lens had cracked or something got onto the negative. But I made a print, all the same.

It gives me the creeps to think of it, even now.

I haven't looked at that photo for thirty years. It's in a shoebox in my darkroom. It was part of a sequence, a succession of shots taken all in a few seconds.

The first couple are good. We had a great angle, even in that weather; a lucky moment when the clouds around us parted, so you can see the road curving away down into the storm behind the rider. But in the last one, the background is different. The clouds appear changed.

There's something on the road behind him. It's out of focus, but it is not a defect in the camera. It is there, behind him, a thing that might have been a cloud or a pall of smoke. But not smoke. Not fog. When I held that photo up to the light to see it properly, I felt something happen: a rush of cold, though the windows were firmly shut. It was as if whatever was in the background had noticed me, was looking at me, out of the photo. For a moment, I felt what Sylvain had described about it: the freezing emptiness that devoured. A hunger, as hard and cold as the void of space.

I know, it sounds stupid. I'm a frightened old man. Why not be scared? My time will be up soon enough. But once or twice a year I have to drive through the mountains at night. And when I do, sometimes I start to feel anxious, for no reason, and I think that I smell something, sharp and sweet and cold. Probably just my car, I know. But it makes me think about that photograph from when I was young, the last photograph of my friend Sylvain T—. When that happens I keep my eyes on the road. I do not look at the darkness to either side, because I fear that if I do, I will see him, racing between the trees, still pedalling for his life, in the grip of a hard white light.

It's not every story set in Scotland that takes place in a sweltering heatwave, but the temperature isn't the only unsettling thing in Philippa East's cautionary tale about the dangers of uncovering the past.

The Archivist

Philippa East

I

I arrived at St Saviour's & George's just as the caretaker was leaving. His motorbike stood roaring in the wide gravelled driveway; I could smell the hot fumes through my open car window.

'Rebecca McMasters?' he shouted over the throb of the engine. 'I was expecting you an hour ago.'

The school stood up tall against the empty blue sky, an expanse of yellow sandstone and flashing windows. I climbed from the car, from one heat to another, catching my breath at the grandeur of the place. My damp skirt was stuck to the backs of my thighs and I wiped a film of sweat from my lip.

'I know... car trouble,' I shouted back. It wouldn't be hard to believe: the car had been on its last legs for months and after the drive up to Scotland, I was surprised it hadn't given up the ghost entirely.

'I've made up rooms for you in the sanatorium, east corridor. You'll find the files and papers in the main office. We stacked them all there.' He tugged his helmet down over his red hair and beard and revved the engine. 'The nearest shop's down in the village. The contractors are due to start tomorrow, so that'll give you tonight to yourself at least.'

Perhaps he was being ironic, I thought. Scottish humour is tricky.

'Won't you be back before then?' I was feeling now the size and emptiness of the place.

The caretaker looked at me through his open visor, a small window. 'No chance. I'll be glad if I never set foot in this place again. Here. Keys.' He tossed the jangling set towards me and I caught them – just.

He gunned his engine and pushed down the visor. The heat from the bike made the air shimmer as he skidded his way towards the gates, kicking up a cloud of gravel behind him. I raised a hand to rub the grit from my eyes. The whine of his engine hung in the air long after he was out of sight; the grounds stretched away to the heavy rows of pine trees that circled the place.

Now there was only me.

The school had been closed for almost five years, but legal wrangling and some court case or other meant that until recently no one had been allowed to touch the place. Now the contractors were moving in, ready to gut the classrooms and offices to make way for luxury flats. Once all trace of the school's history was removed, its past would be too. That's how these things usually worked.

I dragged my suitcase out of the car and locked the boot after me. I wondered whether I should find somewhere tidier to park the old thing, instead of right here in front of the grand entrance. On the other hand, who was here to see? Only the caretaker, kind enough to wait, but gone now too. What I hadn't told him was the real reason for my delay. It was almost too much of a cliché to say out loud: woman pulls over to the side of the road for a crying jag. Anyway, my personal life was none of his business.

I hoisted my suitcase up the steps and passed through the wide doors into the mild cool of inside. The entrance hall's marble flooring was dusty under my feet, and the glass cabinets – once housing pictures and commemorations, awards and trophies – were powdered too with a faint sheen, like a hanging veil. The school had once had a reputation to uphold. Now someone needed to pick over the bones of what was left, and that someone would be me.

The sanatorium was down the east corridor, just as the caretaker had said. The room had a smell familiar to me but which I couldn't quite place: sweet, but sharp – medicinal. I leaned my suitcase against the wall. He'd made up the cot in there in a manly, slapdash way, and left a plug-in kettle and a loose handful of crumpled teabags. A small fridge, the kind students take into halls, held a single pint of skimmed milk; the use-by date today. The caretaker had left me a fan too. I plugged it in and set it whirring, half comforted, half annoyed by its buzzing whine.

In the adjoining room, through a doorless doorway, was a sort of office with a shallow desk in the alcove, along with cupboards and shelving. It was passable as a workspace; I'd certainly known worse. Yes. So far, everything would do. I would bring the files down here, one stack at a time, and sort through them. In this line of work, it's essential to have a system. There's always the temptation on these jobs to rifle through everything where you find it, spilling document after document over the floor as you become engrossed in the secrets you've uncovered. But I've seen where that sort of haphazard approach ends up, and I've learned the hard way the need for a sensible order. I've perfected the art of skimming, taking in as much as I need to know, but never, never getting involved in the nitty-gritty. David says this skill — to never look below the surface of things — can be a curse as well as a blessing. I know what he means, but I don't think I agree.

I sat on the bed and rolled my shoulders to ease out the tension — a legacy of the eight-hour drive, I supposed. There was a bolt too, I noticed now, on the inside of the main door. Despite an uneasy restlessness, an itch to get the job started and finished, I knew I should give myself this evening to rest. Yet the late afternoon sun was magnified by the thick glass and the heat in the room was stifling, even with the fan on its highest setting. I'd forgotten how long it stayed light this far north: it would be another four hours at least before the daylight faded. I stood and tugged at the sash window, but it wouldn't budge and the roller blind was a thin thing, not much good. Outside was greenery and space, room to breathe despite the still air. I locked the san and headed out.

On the front steps, I pushed loose hairs off my forehead and wished I had a hat; dark hair absorbs the sun like nobody's business. But it was cooler out here, in the open air. I could hear the whine of a plane, but when I shaded my eyes and scanned the blue sky, I couldn't see any sign of it. It was hard even to judge in which direction to look. Sometimes the sound seemed to come from low down, behind the trees; a moment later, from directly above. For one brief second, it even felt as if the noise was coming from right beside me, burrowing into my ear.

There was no denying the place was impressive. I didn't know much about the background of St Saviour's & George's, or why this private boys' school had closed so abruptly, everything abandoned. There'd been stories in the newspapers at the time, but news stories are quickly forgotten, and I've never been one to take much interest. I'm not paid enough for that.

I set off through the grounds, round the perimeter of the school. It was strange to think that in this whole school, with dormitories and classrooms for three hundred pupils, not to mention the teachers' quarters, the dining room, the offices, and caretaker's apartments — in this whole grand and echoing place, there was no one but me. Despite the blazing heat, the thought placed a cold fingertip on the ridge of my spine.

I checked my phone, half hoping, half dreading to find a missed call or message from David. Cracks were showing again; we'd parted this morning in the peak of a row, our third in as many weeks. I felt the fissures, but I wasn't prepared to look at them. Instead, I'd done what I always did, what made David angrier than ever: got in the car and left, kidding myself the whole way that I'd good reasons to take this job, a job that was taking me six hundred miles from home and meant I'd be away another whole weekend, a job that was paying me barely enough to cover my petrol money. Kidding myself there was a good reason, other than the need to get away.

I rubbed the corner of my eye, where it still smarted from earlier.

At the back of the school, the grounds sloped gently down, then flattened out some distance away into sports pitches: rugby, athletics, no expense spared.

These kids, a tiny voice whispered on the breeze, *they don't know they're born.*

I frowned to myself, wondering where the words had come from.

I walked closer to the looming walls of the school building, noticing now the signs of wear and tear. The western wall, the one in fullest glare of the sun, had tiny cracks running all across it. As I stared, the wall seemed to come alive before my eyes, rippling, moving, creeping. My heart shot up in my chest, but I caught myself the way I'd been taught, and forced myself to look closer, look properly. I let out my breath in a rush of relief when I realised what it was: tiny scorpions, warmed by the sun, scuttling across the sandstone, right at home.

Back in the san, I fished a packet of instant noodles from the bottom of my suitcase and put the kettle on. Instant noodles are a godsend on jobs like these. But now I realised I had no bowl — or fork for that matter. I poked about the shelves of the office, dislodging boxes of plasters, packs of tissues, thermometers: all sensible nursing stock, but not what I was after. In the corner was the wooden cupboard, more like a wardrobe for clothes than for medical devices or pupils' sick charts. Perhaps this was where the school nurse had kept her stash of naughty cigarettes, confiscated from the boys. Perhaps in here too, she'd stash a bowl or plate, for guilty feasts on nights when she couldn't sleep. The kettle began to keen, air squeezing through some crack in its plastic lid and its spout filling the room with bursts of hot steam. I grasped the cupboard's wooden door handles, half expecting the thing to be locked, but the panels clicked open easily enough.

From behind the doors a face, a head, stared back at me.

II

The kettle was shrieking, like a child with pins stuck in it. I felt like shrieking too, in anger at having been given such a scare. It was just a stupid doll, and a hideous one at that: thick brown braids and a yellow tartan dress. A frilly tam-o'-shanter was perched on top of its porcelain head, stuck on with a thistle pin, and the doll's hands were clasped in front of her. When I gave her a poke, the arms swung side to side in a crude parody of rock-a-bye-baby.

What on earth was this thing doing in the nurse's cupboard? Perhaps she used it to frighten the boys.

Don't be naughty, lads, or Wee Jeanie'll get you.

In a perverse fit of rebellion, I lifted the doll down from the shelf and set her on the table by the bed.

The kettle clicked off and I poured the water over broken noodles in the best container I could find: a coffee mug. The noodles were bland and full of chemicals, but on my empty stomach they would do just fine. I drank them like soup, staring as I ate at the doll that had scared me so much only a moment ago. She wasn't such an ugly-looking creature, I thought now. That yellow dress was doing nothing for her, but she had the plump cheeks and paint-shined eyes of any self-respecting dolly. I tipped up the mug again and frowned, almost scalding myself. Amongst the frills of her tartan dress, caught in the puffed sleeves above the little clasped hands, something was stuck. At first glance it looked like a marble, blue and whorled. But as I looked closer, I saw that there was some sort of crumpled wrapper in there too. I set the mug down and reached forward. With finger and thumb I fished out the object.

A boiled sweet.

And at the moment it dislodged into my fingers, I heard a sound, sharp and blunt.

Clack.

For a moment I thought the door catch had slipped, that the bolt had sprung loose and snapped open. But the door stood closed and the keys I'd left in the lock hadn't moved. The sound didn't repeat. Perhaps I was imagining things. But I recognised now the smell that permeated the san. Aniseed.

I placed the sweet carefully on the bedside table: blue, boiled, crinkle-wrapped.

It was still daylight when I settled into bed that evening and I read for a while by the light seeping through the thin blind. The fan droned on, doing little to cool the air. I'd tried again to lift the ancient sash window, but it was stuck fast.

I must have drifted off eventually, because when I woke, it wasn't sunlight but moonlight that was seeping into the room. My book, a tatty second-hand paperback, had fallen on the floor and I must have kicked away the blankets in the heat because they too had slithered off the bed. The smell of aniseed was thick in the air; and in the moonlight, the doll's face next to me on the bedside table had taken on a crooked, lopsided look, as if someone had painted on a sneer.

I switched the bedside lamp on and the little rosebud mouth and plump cheeks returned.

I lay back on the flat pillow and looked at her. She regarded me silently, giving nothing away. I left the lamp on and closed my eyes. There was no sound but the groan of the fan. I lay there feeling the breeze, seeing the moonlight through my eyelashes. The fan made a soft knocking, its mechanism clunking each time it rotated.

Half awake, half asleep, I can't tell if I spoke aloud or only thought the question inside my own head: 'Who's there?'

The knocking came again, a little harder this time; now it sounded like a small hand tapping at the door, soft but persistent, and with it came words I can only have imagined: *Go away, go away, go away.*

And then a quick, bright thought, the last before I fell into the full dark of sleep: *Scorpions? But there would be no scorpions here.*

In the morning I woke early. The heat was back with a vengeance.

I made myself a milky tea from the supplies the caretaker had left and got down to work. The night had been hazy, full of strange dreams. I wondered what time the contractors and workmen would arrive, and in the same moment, I realised I hadn't called David. I sent him a hurried text: *arrived safe, heat up here is something else.* I tried to think of something more to say, something a bit more forgiving, but the stubborn part of me wasn't ready yet to apologise.

The files in the main staff office were easy enough to find. The cabinets had been broken open long before and the usual stuff lay in piles throughout the room. Insurance policies, class timetables, and minutes from staff meetings. Plus the files on each pupil, all two hundred and eighty-three of them. I took the largest stacks I could carry down to the sanatorium and set them out on the desk in the little office room. To begin with I put the fan on, but it blew the papers around too much. Instead I stripped off down to my vest top and hitched my skirt up as high as was decent. Every half an hour or so, I'd make my way to the main school office and bring another armful back.

With the window closed and the fan off, the smell of aniseed was stronger than ever. The smell seemed to come from the doll, probably something to do with the sweet stuffed in her dress. I looked around now for the little blue candy, but couldn't spot it anywhere. Perhaps it had rolled under the bed or I'd thrown it out with last night's rubbish. I made a mental note to get down to the village today. I couldn't keep living on instant noodles. I knew myself, and how engrossed I could get in a job. The brain needs calories too. If I got in supplies for breakfasts and lunches, then I could have dinners in a nearby pub; there must be one around here somewhere.

As I worked, I felt my knots of tension ease. This is dull work, but it suits me: putting these documents in some sense of order, for someone else to decide what to keep or throw away. In all these piles and stacks of paper, only two things caught my attention.

Firstly, in every pupil's file, near the back, there was a section marked off by a red divider. This section was labelled Discipline. In every case, this section was empty and appeared to have been hastily cleared: little scraps of paper still clung to the binders.

The second thing was the dates: dates of birth that let me calculate the boys' ages. Nineteen the oldest and the youngest, six.

He didn't stand a chance, the little voice said.

In the space at the back of my eyes I could feel the creepings of a headache. This heat, it was relentless. When I pressed my palms to my eyes, spots danced behind my eyelids. And sitting there, at the desk in the alcove, blind for a moment, that's when I heard it. Faint, warbling. If I hadn't had such sharp ears I might have mistaken it for bird song. But when I thought about it, I hadn't seen any birds round here, not even a sparrow. So it wasn't bird song, but it was singing.

I opened my eyes. The tune was louder now. Like the smell of aniseed, it was one I recognised from long ago, from when I lived up here, when I was a kid. I could make out the words now.

> *Ally bally, ally-bally bee*
> *Sittin' on yer mammie's knee*
> *Greetin' for a wee bawbie*
> *Tae buy some Coulter's Candy*

It's a radio, I told myself, someone's left a radio on somewhere, some local station, playing Scottish folk songs. Or one of the workmen has arrived; it's someone outside, whistling, singing to themselves.

I did a stupid thing then. I shouted hello, as if there really was someone else there in that deserted school, someone I could blame for that eerie song. The pounding in my head was worse now, and that pounding was saying *the doll, the doll*.

I got up from the desk, scraping back my chair, pulling myself round the edges of the doorway. I got there just as the music stopped and the doll's arms swung back to where they belonged, hands clasped innocently in her lap. And I almost could have believed that I'd imagined the whole thing, that it was the heat and the headache confusing me, setting my imagination running wild, if in the next moment I didn't hear that heart-pinching clack, and see that blue boiled sweet tumble out of the sleeves of the yellow dress, hard as a stone, as if she was trying to throw it at me.

I grabbed my purse and the car keys, and got outside to the car. The engine was sluggish to start, and as I sat there turning and turning the ignition, the engine overheated and protesting, it felt like the whole school was leaning down over me, pressing down on the top of my head. I didn't dare look up, dreading what I might see staring from those glassy windows. At last the ignition caught and I gunned the engine and wrenched the car round the gravel drive. I didn't breathe properly until I was out of those gates, and beyond the perimeter of pine trees; in fact I didn't breathe easy until I'd driven all the way to the village and parked in an ordinary-looking car park, with ordinary-looking people going about their business all around me.

Stupid, so stupid.

I went to a cafe and ordered a sandwich. My stomach clenched at the first few bites: I hadn't felt how hungry I was. *Skipping breakfast*, I could hear David's voice saying, *come on, Rebecca, you know that's not good*. I ate and I made myself think, picking apart my confusion, my panic. You're jumping, I told myself, you're assuming. Wait, think, take it step by step.

Logic swam back to me in a cool wave. The doll, of course, was a wind-up doll that sang and swung, dispensing sweeties.

The key must not have been fully unwound, and had slipped and played the song. It explained the sweetie I'd found last night, and the other one that had emerged with a clack this morning.

And the scorpions? a different voice in my head asked. Well of course they weren't scorpions, they were lizards. Scuttling in the heat, and hiding away in the cool of the morning. Lizards. An easy mistake to make.

I finished the whole sandwich and went to the store. I stocked up on bread, cheese, cereal, milk — enough to see me through the next few days. The store had air conditioning and I stood in the freezer aisle for as long as I could, letting its cool sink into my skin. When I returned to the car, my old banger, the world felt calmer. I had obligations. I had a job, I was a professional.

I put the food in the boot, and drove back.

My phone jittered as I turned up the driveway, but stopped before I could pull up. David's picture showed on the screen. I parked in front of the school and pressed the recall button, noticing how quickly my heart was beating.

David's voice, when he answered, was brisk and gruff. 'Rebecca?'

'Just missed you. I was driving back from the village.'

'We said we'd check in. I need to know how you're doing.'

The distance down the line felt vast and echoey. I climbed out of the car, the phone in one hand, keys in the other. 'Oh, you know. It's really hot.'

'Yes, you said.'

Right. My text. I retrieved the shopping from the back of the car and locked the doors behind me. 'There's just me here at the moment,' I went on, 'but I've already got started.'

'That's good.'

'Yep.'

There was a pause.

'I'm sorry about before,' he said. Sometimes David apologises on my behalf. It's a sort of arrangement we've come to.

I climbed the steps into the atrium. 'It doesn't matter,' I told him. 'Not now.'

'So when do you think you'll be up there till?'

'Monday morning at the latest, I hope.'

There was another silence on the line as I walked down the corridor towards the san. Then: 'Rebecca? How about I come join you? We could spend the rest of the weekend together, some of next week. I could book us a nice hotel. You know, make a little holiday of it.'

The headache from this morning was starting up again.

Don't let him come here.

I shook my head to clear the thought.

'Could do,' I said carefully.

'Will you think about it at least?'

I could feel the disappointment through the handset. The gap between us stretched a few miles wider. Too wide. I gripped the phone.

'David —' I blurted. 'I found this doll.'

'This what?'

'A doll. There's a doll here, in the room where I'm sleeping.'

'Okay...' David's voice was cautious. 'Well, maybe it belonged to one of the boarders.'

I pictured her: frills, plaits, rosebud mouth. 'I don't think so... David, it sings a nursery rhyme. Coulter's Candy.'

'Coulter's Candy, huh?'

Make him shut up.

I shook my head again and pinched the bridge of my nose.

'Look, never mind. I don't know why I'm telling you this.'

'Rebecca, it's alright. We should talk, you can talk to me – '

'It's nothing, it's stupid. Look I'll ring you later.'

And I hung up.

Inside the san, I put the shopping bags down on the floor. I was breathing hard and could almost feel my pulse in my mouth. The doll was right there where I'd left her, still and silent. I lifted her up and felt through the layers of her dress, the ribbons and bows at the back, until finally, thankfully, my fingers closed upon what I'd hoped to find all along: the wind-up key.

I sank down on the bed, shivering with relief. That was all she was. A wind-up doll, with a mechanism that slipped.

I grasped the key and twisted it, unwinding its coils. The familiar tune started up again and the stiff arms swung back and forth.

Poor wee Jeanie was gettin' awfy thin,
A rickle o' bones covered ower wi' skin...

I kept up the pressure on the key, turning every last note out of it. I kept it turning until it wouldn't turn any more. No chance of it slipping now. I put her back where I'd found her and shut the cupboard doors tight. I texted David: *I'm alright.*

I made myself a coffee this time, strong and black.

Then I got back to work.

The next morning I was woken by my phone. It was the caretaker, ringing to tell me the workmen were postponing for a week. Did I need anything, he asked. Would I be alright there on my own?

I sat up in bed and shrugged. 'Why wouldn't I be?'

There was a silence on the line, like he was waiting for me to take my words back. When I didn't say anything else he grunted and hung up.

It was too hot to eat any breakfast and I knew if I didn't push on with the work this morning, the headache that was lurking behind my eyes would be here too soon for me to work much past lunchtime. Once again, I carried stacks of papers and files from the main office to the san and sifted through them one by one. Painstaking work, but it was me at my best.

St Saviour's & George's, it seemed, had been an exemplary school. Unruly behaviour was rarely a problem. The older boys helped the teachers to keep things in hand.

He let Jenks's scorpion out. Prize pet scorpion.

I didn't know where these thought fragments were coming from. It was like someone kept twiddling a radio knob in my head, picking up random bandwidths.

Scorpions again though, I noted.

At lunchtime I had another coffee. The headache somehow was keeping at bay. It was so quiet here. No workmen, no wind. I'm not sure quite where the impulse came from, in fact I hardly even realised what I was doing until it was done, and the doll had been rescued from the cupboard and was resting once again on the bedside table, smiling softly with her little red mouth.

She was sitting there when I found the letter. The one from the local hospital doctor to the school nurse, Miss Aitkins. He hoped he was not speaking out of turn, he wrote, but he was concerned about the recent referrals. He knew lads could be lads, rowdy and clumsy at the best of times, but the injuries he had been asked to treat, perhaps they had another cause, did Miss Aitkin catch his drift?

Clipped to this letter so neatly typed on official hospital stationery, was a sheet of writing paper, Miss Aitkin's own it seemed, for there was no school letterhead.

Dear Doctor, said its hand-written scrawl, *I would beg you not to question –*

And there it ended.

Come high afternoon, it was simply too hot to work. I snapped elastic bands round the papers that were still lying lose, and switched on the fan. I stripped down to my underwear, lay flat on the bed and closed my eyes. My sleep was a thick weight. When I woke, my mouth was parched like a wrung-out sponge. I was dehydrated, I realised. I hadn't been drinking properly in all this heat.

I lay there hardly breathing, facing the wall, not turning round. I slid my hand under the pillow to where my phone was, to where I always kept it these days when I slept.

Right away I called David. He didn't pick up the first time, but instead of leaving a message, I kept ringing. Ringing and ringing.

When at last he answered, there was such a noise in the background, a thrumming, like he was in a train or a car.

Despite the racket, I spoke in a whisper. 'David?'

'Rebecca – what is it?'

Still without turning over I held the phone up in the hot air above my shoulder.

> *Ally bally, ally-bally bee*
> *Crawlin' roond on hand an' knee...*

I pressed the phone back to my ear. 'Can't you hear it? Tell me you can hear it.'

'Hear what? Rebecca –'

'Turn that noise off. Listen!'

...Begging to yer poor mammie
Tae gi' you Coulter's Candy

The song was loud, wailing. I didn't remember this verse. I didn't know these words.

'Rebecca?' His voice was so blurred, so crackly. Where was he, what was he doing?

'Listen!' I hissed. 'Listen!'

I held the phone there, until I was sure he'd have heard, then wrenched myself over in the bed, forcing myself once again to look, to really *see*, like everyone kept telling me.

When I turned over the doll was silent. Stock still.

I threw down the phone and grabbed her by her frilly dress and tried to find the key that wound her up but even though I searched and searched and in the end turned her right upside down so her skirts fell over her head, there was no sign of the mechanism that had reassured me so much.

The line was clearer when I picked up the phone again.

'Rebecca, what is it?' Miles away, I heard him trying to stay calm. 'What am I supposed to hear?'

I sat down on the bed and took a deep breath. 'Nothing. There's... nothing there.'

David's voice came to me across a long, long distance. 'Rebecca, please. I think you know what this is.'

My head was pounding. 'What?'

'I found your medication. You left it at home –'

Clack.

I hung up.

III

I didn't take a single break in my work for the rest of the day. I had to get it finished. My headache was stinging my eyes, but I worked on through, unearthing more secrets that I filed to one side, in a careful bundle that I marked only The San. There were pieces coming together, stories joining up, but I worked like an automaton, taking nothing in, for none of this was mine, and none of these failures had been my fault.

About eleven I reached the end. I took everything back to the main office and lined it up neatly, filed in the archivist's system, ready to be disposed of or kept at will. Back in the san, I fell exhausted onto the bed, without even properly undressing. I hadn't had a wash, I realised, for three days now.

I did fall asleep, despite the heat; I mean I must have done because of the nightmare. I say it was a nightmare now, but part of me still wonders if it wasn't real, if everything that happened to me in that school wasn't real, though the doctor later put it all down to another episode, brought on by heatstroke and lack of food.

I dreamed, or I woke; what difference does it make? In sleep or in waking I was sitting upright in the bed, my legs stuck out straight before me. The doll was there on the bedside table, a caricature of me, or me of it, my hands clasped and my arms moved by a force outside of me, swinging from side to side.

I was a puppet, a doll, a robot, and then the knocking came, and it was knocking, but it was a clacking too, and I saw sweet after sweet come rolling out of the doll: from her sleeves, her hair, her skirts, her mouth. They fell out and rolled off the table and the floor was covered with them, like a sea of marbles; if you tried to walk on them you'd break your legs.

I was sitting up and I was lying down and in the dream I was sick, but in other dreams I was the nurse, and the knocking went on and I knew I should get up and open the door, I knew who was on the other side, I knew what the doctor had warned of in his letter and what a teacher had raised in a report, and what in the end I had turned a blind eye to.

Knock, clack, knock, clack, and my arms swung back and forth with a life of their own and the doll swung and sang, and knocked and clacked, and through it all, my head pressed into the pillow, I felt the pressure building. A sweet was pushing, pushing out against my ribcage, it was pushing to burst my own lungs, and I knew if I let the boy in what I would see, the haemorrhage that didn't show on the outside, but he'd complained of stomach pains and said he couldn't breathe, and if I opened the door, there'd be no getting away from what had happened to him: no accident of course, but the brutal beating in the dormitory, by Jenks and all his friends, for letting the scorpion out. And the pain in my head shrieked:

Open the door!

Don't open the door!

The doctor!

The nurse!

You told them not to be naughty! You told them, Wee Jeanie warned!

I couldn't breathe, but I must have screamed, and then the sanatorium door handle turned and the sanatorium door was opening.

When I came to, it was broad daylight. I was lying on my side on the bed in the sanatorium, and David was there. He propped me up and held a mug of water to my mouth.

'I finished it, David. The work's all done.'

'Drink. Just keep drinking.' He slipped a pill in with the water too.

I looked around for the doll. There was no sign of her. Through in the little office, the cupboard doors were tight closed.

'I read about it,' said David. 'What happened here. The beatings, the violence.'

'The boy,' I said. 'He was only six.'

'Yes.'

'He died.'

'That's right. Outside the nurse's office. The caretaker found him.'

'She knew,' I said. 'She knew, that's the worst thing. But she didn't do anything. Her door was locked.'

David let that one go. 'I've arranged an appointment for you. When we get home.'

I closed my eyes and let the tears slide down my nose. I nodded.

He helped me up. He'd already packed my suitcase, thrown away the food, and the floor was clear, I noticed. There were no sweets.

'Did you find the doll?' I asked.

David shook his head.

Outside, the air was so still, the world looked like a photograph. David's car was parked beside mine.

'We can leave yours,' he said. 'I've spoken to a friend, he'll come pick it up.'

He opened the passenger door and helped me in. It was only when I sank into the cracked leather that I realised how weak and sick I felt. I couldn't think of the last time I'd eaten, and there was

a whining ring in my ears, the kind I got when my blood pressure
was low and my iron levels were through the floor. I dropped my
face into my hands. No wonder, I thought, that I'd had such bad
dreams. No wonder I had been hallucinating.

And the pills, I'd stopped the pills. How many times, the same
thing. I felt like crying.

David loaded my suitcase into the boot, and then climbed into
the driver's seat beside me. His movements, his body, were so
familiar to me, I felt a choking rush of love, the kind I hadn't felt
in weeks. He had come, he'd seen what I couldn't, he'd broken
my fall, like every other time before.

David started the engine and set the air con on full. I shut
my eyes, waiting for the jolt as we pulled away, the haunting over,
going home.

I opened my eyes. We hadn't moved. David was staring in
the rear-view mirror, staring at something, I couldn't tell what. I
reached out for him. 'What is it?'

The sun was a glare on the windscreen, the seatbelt was tight
across my chest. David shook his head, like shaking something
away. I twisted and craned my neck to see, looking over my
shoulder, back at St Saviour's & George's. I passed a hand in
front of my eyes, my vision unsteady and blurred. What was it,
that thing? It was like a small creature, a mouse or spider, moving
jerkily down the steps as if being pushed or pulled, moving like
that though there wasn't a breath of wind.

As it came nearer, I made out the colour – blue – and the
texture – crinkled.

A sweetie paper.

David wrenched the handbrake, released the clutch.

'Let's get out of here,' he said.

*Richard Agemo's story takes an atmospheric look at
the bonds we form with the houses where we spend our
lives; and, perhaps, the bonds they form with us.*

The House Friends

Richard Agemo

The ear exams, hearing tests, and MRI scans turned up nothing.
The problem is psychological. My shrink wants me to write down
everything and read it at our next session, but I wish she would
stop calling it ringing in the ears. Because it's not ringing, but
whirling — like when you're in the dentist's chair but louder, and
just in the right ear, not the one turned to my neighbour Carmen
when she screamed in the barn.

I had often mused about buying the rural home I grew up in.
The two-story house my father built sits on five breezy acres in
central Illinois. Though it's well built, the house isn't perfect.
The window beneath the north apex of the roof tilts slightly,
as if something's pulling it to the interior, which I found
charming. To me as a boy, the house was a palace that attracted
and replenished the most precious things: hummingbirds and

swallows, my mother's peonies, and vast grass lawns that appear in my dreams to this day.

Father built a barn too, planted an orchard, and dug up a meadow for a pond. He called the place Windy Acres.

My first memory: chasing butterflies when I was five, the house watching over me and sharing my joy. Isolation, my therapist says, helps explain how I started to think of the house as something alive. While my sisters played with girls who lived up the road, the closest boys my age lived miles away in Hudson, a small town.

I was satisfied with being a college professor in Chicago, but when the opportunity arose to buy the house, I had the chance to recapture something I'd cherished and lost. Still, having spent years in Chicago, I asked myself, did I truly wish to live in the country? This question revolved around memories of my fifteenth birthday, when my parents told me we were moving to Normal, a college town a half-hour from Windy Acres. I felt devastated, as though I were losing a friend. On the morning we left, I walked the grounds saying farewell in tears.

I resented the new owner at first. Like my parents, Frank Speery and his wife had a son and two daughters. Depressed as I was, I saw them as thieves. Father asked Frank if I might camp there occasionally. Frank, a sympathetic man, said he'd welcome me.

Three months after the Speerys moved, Frank's eleven-year-old son, Erik, drowned in the pond. The pier Father built had become dilapidated, and a plank broke when Erik ran onto it, causing him to fall into the water and strike his head on a rock. I felt ashamed, not because Father had never fixed the pier, but because I had disparaged the Speerys for buying the house.

Nine weeks ago I saw Frank Speery alive for the last time. Seventy-five and grey bearded, he wore stiff denim overalls. I thanked him for keeping the promise he made to me twenty-five summers ago, when he let me camp two nights at Windy Acres. I had brought a telescope and, by the end of my visit, decided to study astronomy. I remember standing with Frank on the house stoop, waiting for Father to come and take me back to Normal. With a bent brow, Frank told me he knew I liked the place, and that someday I would want to own a home. He promised I'd have the first chance to buy the house if he ever sold.

During breaks from college at the University of Illinois, I often drove to see my family and then to see Frank. Only once did he talk about his son's death. Erik and his fly rod were found at the bottom of the shallow end of the pond, his baseball cap floating on the surface. The impact on the rock gashed his forehead and broke his nose, turning his face purple. Frank told me all this in a quiet, matter-of-fact way, never letting on how much Erik's death bothered him. Frank worked a lot on the pier, replacing the planks, weatherproofing them, and adding a railing – his way of coping with Erik's death, I thought.

My visits ended when I began teaching astrophysics in Chicago, the start of my time of troubles, which included a divorce, a series of rebound relationships, and the death of my parents. For five years I didn't see Frank or speak with him. Then one summer he called me on my faculty line. In the last year, he had lost his wife and his daughters had moved away. He wanted to sell half of the property, including the pond, to the Gridleys, a couple in their twenties. Remembering his promise, he was checking with me first. That Frank hadn't forgotten made me happy. He was keeping the house, the orchard and the barn, the things I liked most. I told him I had no problem with the partial sale.

In August I went to see him. A split-rail fence now divided the property, and the frame of Bryan and Carmen Gridley's new house had risen. Bryan, a gregarious cowboy-type, boomed a frequent laugh that shook his full beard. He worked nights as a doctor in the ER at a hospital in Bloomington, which is next to Normal. His tan boots came up to the middle of his calves, the leather gleaming as if he polished them every hour, catching light even in shadows.

Carmen, his Dutch-born wife, painted landscapes. She had platinum blonde hair, peaceful green eyes, and wore crimson lipstick that exploded on her mouth. Her English was excellent, rarely marred by an accent.

The four of us sat on Frank's patio drinking beer. Frank went inside for a moment, leaving me with Bryan and Carmen. I nodded at the pond in the distance. The noon sun had turned the water to silver.

'I see there's a chain blocking the entrance to the pier,' I said.

'Frank thinks the posts are rotten, Ed,' Bryan answered. I had introduced myself as Edward Rymes; he assumed I didn't mind being called Ed, but I didn't correct him. He took a swig then said, 'Farm kids play on the pier.' A nervous edge tinged his voice. Something told me he was lying.

'But it's your pond, your pier now, right?' I said.

Ignoring my question, he put down his empty bottle and looked towards the barn. 'Frank's thinking about turning the barn into a B&B. With Lake Bloomington and the commercial vineyard nearby, there's potential. Carmen would help manage it, so she's not just painting all the time. Right, love?'

'I don't paint all the time.' She directed her words to me and our eyes met. 'Sometimes I like something different.'

Her irises matched the colour of the lawn stretched out before us, which struck me as remarkable, as if the landscapes she painted had dyed her eyes, while the colour of her lips recalled the wild strawberries I had once devoured. Our gazes locked just long enough to tempt me. But the Gridleys were now Frank's friends, something I wasn't about to screw up.

Maybe I should have. Things might have been different. Maybe Carmen and I would have run off together, she would have had no reason to scream, and I wouldn't need a psychologist. Just like me. Trying to escape the past through some new fantasy.

I went back the next year, during spring break. The Gridley's house was finished, ready for a summer visit from Carmen's father from the Netherlands. Frank, Bryan, and I painted the barn red. Frank talked more about a B&B and wondered if it should have one, two, or three bedrooms. He and Bryan mused about a sand beach and a deck as upgrades to the pond. The chain was down, and from the patio we watched kids fishing from the pier. I'd seen them there during morning walks, and at dusk when I set up my telescope.

One evening I saw a kid with his fly reel whizzing his line over and over again in the same spot. The blue hat he wore had the 'C' for the Cubs. For fun, I pointed my telescope in his direction, but he left before I could focus.

One other thing sticks with me about that visit: the small upset with Frank at the barn. When I walked under a ladder, Frank told me I shouldn't, and I laughed. 'Frank, you know I don't believe that crap.' He seemed hurt, grimacing with a sideways glance.

In September he called to say he was selling his half of the property. The upkeep was proving too much and he was moving to Hudson. He was conflicted about keeping his promise to me — he had another anxious buyer: Carmen's father.

Dr Egbert de Groeshe was a retired dentist from Haarlem in the Netherlands. While visiting Carmen and Bryan in July, he'd become smitten with Windy Acres. By Frank's measured words, I could tell he faced a dilemma: either keep his promise and sell to me at fair market value, or renege and sell to a close relative of neighbours who were also his friends.

'Maybe I should come and talk with the Gridleys,' I suggested to Frank. 'See if we can work something out.'

On the train from Chicago, as muddy harvested fields flew by, a plan formed in my mind. In all the years I'd known Frank, the subject of my resources never came up. To get the divorce over with, I paid my ex off with most of my savings, while holding on to a crazy investment in radio frequencies a colleague convinced me to buy. It was worth nothing at the time but in five years yielded millions. If I could have done things over, I would have bought the house from Frank earlier and leased it back to him. Now he was stuck. To help him out, if need be, I could buy his property and the Gridleys' at a premium and reunite the two parcels.

The train pulled into Normal and I rented a car. In the twinkling afternoon, I drove north out of town. A half hour later, after passing endless barren cornfields, I sighted the old house a quarter-mile away. I felt elated. As I've explained in therapy, growing up I loved the house and, turning into the driveway, I had the sensation it loved me too, and wanted me back.

My therapist suggested I write about my lonely childhood, how I immersed myself in fantasies, and explore the possibility I'm still imagining things. The childhood we've gone over several times before, in detail, and frankly I see no sense in going over it again. The problem (for the five hundredth time) began the night in the barn with Carmen, when the lights went out and she screamed. Until then I enjoyed perfect hearing. Maybe I'll go back there and face my demons, and then maybe I won't — fear does serve a healthy purpose, you know.

Frank and the Gridleys greeted me after I got out of the car. We went to the patio. The new deck on the pond was done. A youngster — the same one I'd seen in the spring — was casting his fly rod.

'So what are we going to do here?' Bryan said to me after his second beer. No laugh followed, not even a smile, and his flat tone surprised me.

'How do you mean?' I took a sip from my bottle.

Bryan crossed his legs so I saw the black sole of one of his boots. 'Frank says he promised to sell to you, but we want this place.' He turned to Carmen. 'Don't we, love?'

She shifted to me. 'Bryan means my dad wants to buy the house.' Pausing to look at Frank, she raised her brow as if to gain his support; but Frank, who sat between me and the Gridleys, just stared at his shoes.

An autumn gust ruffled Carmen's blonde bangs as she turned back to me. 'You see, Edward, Dad is retired, and with Frank's departure, this way he can live near me and Bryan.' She flashed a smile. 'Frank told us you have odder ideas.'

I knew she meant 'other ideas,' not 'odder,' but my own smile was forced. 'Carmen, I grew up here, in the house my father built. It's like a friend. Owning it has been my dream.'

'Well, of course, I understand.' Her eyes narrowed into a squint as she nodded. I glanced at her hands. One clutched the wrist of the other, trembling. 'But my dad can't live with us,' she added. 'Another house will ruin our property. Father wants Frank's house. He's not even sixty, you know, very active, and he'll renovate.'

'Dr de Groeshe is still pretty good with a drill,' Bryan said and laughed. 'Come on, Ed, let the old man have the house. He'll take good care of it, won't he, Frank?'

I thought of walls being torn down, fixtures being pulled out like teeth, and a new wall going up, dividing the long living room that spanned the north side of the house. That room was my favourite, its dark green carpet and light green walls with windows facing the pond, barn, and orchard, breathing in the outdoors. As a boy I would always tread carefully in that pristine space, taking off my shoes, moving slowly, respecting its beauty. Now I feared it would be radically altered, transformed into something I wouldn't recognize.

'What about the barn?' Bryan asked. 'Why not renovate it for my father-in-law?'

The question sounded rehearsed, the Gridleys' Plan B. I looked towards the red building a few hundred yards away, once more pulled into my childhood: climbing the fragrant bales of hay stacked in the adjoining shed, riding Victor at a gallop, brushing Old Red. Frank quit boarding horses long ago. Last time I was in there, tools were everywhere, some holding down architectural drawings of the B&B spread out on a table. Fishing rods lined one wall, a few of which belonged to Erik, Frank said. Now, after hearing the Gridleys' Plan B, I hated the idea of changing anything about the barn, not even the dirt floor.

'The barn,' Carmen said, acting her part, grinning widely. 'Why, of course.'

I felt a hole in my stomach and took a chug from my bottle. I loathed the idea of losing the barn, my favourite childhood haunt. I felt a little stubborn, even mean. 'Frank's still the owner,' I said. 'It's his decision.' Frank frowned and then, just as I was about to float my proposal to buy everyone out, Bryan leaned forward.

'Okay, how about this.'

Great, I thought. *Plan C.*

'Divide the property into two tracts, one with the house and one with the barn, and auction them separately.' Bryan looked at his shimmering boots, squinted, and looked up again. 'The sole bidders would be you and Carmen's father. You'll both have a shot at buying the house, the barn, or both.'

Frank raised his face, his slow nod indicating he liked the suggestion. I had no idea whether he'd listened to Bryan's 'solution' in advance. It didn't matter. They might have been thinking that Dr de Groesch could win at least one of the two auctions. With my resources, I knew he couldn't.

Carmen tilted her head at me and raised her dark eyebrows. Hiding my satisfaction, I kept a blank face. 'Agreed,' I said bluntly.

The corners of Bryan's mouth crept up through his beard.

We set the first day in October, a Monday three weeks away, as the auction date. After we stood and raised a toast, my eyes scanned the lawn. An oak planted by my father now towered thirty feet in the air, its splendid orange, red, and yellow leaves mesmerising. You will live here, it seemed to chant to me. I pointed my bottle towards the pond. 'Just who is that kid?'

Carmen fixed her gaze on him. 'Probably his parents tell him not to come here, but I don't let him bodder me. He'll never say his name.'

I put down my bottle and stood. 'Let's see about that.'

I walked off the patio. The kid wore the same Cubs hat, shading his face from the September sun. As I strode to the pond, he swung around and ran off the deck, rod over shoulder, climbed a grassy embankment then disappeared into the forest. 'Wait!' I shouted and thrust my hand in the air.

When I turned back, Frank was gone, but Bryan and Carmen were watching me from the patio. Suddenly they began picking up bottles, cleaning up as if nothing had happened. A breeze caught a paper napkin zigzagging crazily in the air. Giving chase, I caught it, crumpling it in my hand as I stepped on the patio.

'See, I told you,' Carmen said, her back to me as she picked up a bottle. 'Don't let the kid bodder you.'

Frank put me up for the night. In the morning, before I returned to Chicago, I found Carmen painting in the orchard. She put down her brush, then wiped her hands on her paint-smeared smock. 'My dad wants to speak to you, Edward. Will you talk with him on the phone this week?'

I glanced at her canvas. The orchard, its colours swirling like a galaxy, trapped a child who was clawing at my father's house that loomed in the background. The painting scared me. I looked at her again. Her beauty scared me. Even her question scared me.

'What does he want to talk about?'

'He's a nice man.' Her strawberry lips folded into each other for a moment then released. 'But he can be emotional. When I told him I didn't want him living with us, there were tears. But it's best for everyone. Solitude is the reason we came here. It helps me, my painting ... as long as no one's disturbing me.'

'Your dad agreed to the auction, right?' I said.

'Yes, he agreed. I don't know why he wants to speak to you. He won't say.'

'Does Bryan know?'

She drifted towards me until our faces were inches apart. I caught her scent; rather, it caught me: rose mixed with a woody fragrance, natural and wild, her emerald eyes staring at my astonished face. I saw her as a creature of the orchard, its waiflike custodian destined to roam forever among the fruit whose faithful return every summer was a joy of my childhood. For an instant I felt an urge to ignore the splatters of oil paint and place my hands on her waist, unsure whether to pull her closer to me or push her away. I heard myself breathing.

'Edward, I respect my dad, but can only take him in small doses. He makes me crazy.'

'Sounds pretty severe.'

'He's too protective, always telling me to be careful, the same way he treated mother. He promises to stop but he doesn't. I refuse to let him live with us, but Bryan took his side. Now they're pushing the idea of making the barn my dad's home, but

I don't want that, either. Bryan's forcing me to accept it and act like I want it.'

'Forcing you how?'

She wouldn't tell me. The morning was chilly, and though I wore a jacket over a wool sweater, I shivered. 'How is Bryan pressuring you?' I persisted.

'Someone should be here, he says, to help keep a watch on things. All right, I get that, but no, not my dad. I won't be turned into a child.' She turned to her painting. 'He ruins my art. Sometimes I'd just like to run away!' Darting around to me again, she brought her hands to my shoulders, squeezing them. 'Edward, you are going to win both auctions, aren't you?'

Too stunned to answer, I removed her hands from my shoulders, stepped back, and collected myself. It was as if she and the orchard were one, and now they were trapping *me*.

'What do you want me to tell him?' I stammered.

'No matter what he offers, Edward, please don't let him buy any part of Windy Acres. *Please.*'

Her desperation puzzled me. She sounded as if keeping her father away was for someone's physical protection, possibly mine.

'Have him call me at the University in Chicago.' I gave her the number.

On the train I reconsidered my scheme, fearing Carmen would be too much to deal with. Would I let that direct my decision, stop me from achieving a goal I'd envisioned for decades? No. I was going to win both auctions and buy *all* of Frank's property.

On the phone, Dr de Groesch chuckled a lot. He told me he loved the house and could pay more than its actual value. Then he made a peculiar offer: he and I would share the house, one of us living upstairs, the other downstairs. And I could have the barn.

'Dr de Groesch, I'm sorry, but I prefer we stick with the auction, what's best for Frank Speery.'

A long silence followed until the doctor whispered goodbye and hung up. Later, I thought I could have been more polite. Perhaps Carmen's influence caused my abrupt reply, even if I hadn't been thinking of her at the time.

Frank held the auction by conference call in his house. Bryan and Carmen sat with him by the phone. In fifteen minutes it was over. 'Hope there are no hard feelings,' I said, but the doctor only muttered his thanks to Frank and dropped off the call. Relief ran through me. I had won playing fair — at least fair enough. In eight days, my agent closed with Frank, who had bought a place in Hudson. He rented a truck to haul his furniture, leaving everything else to me, including the tools in the barn.

In the third week of October, I moved. The first night there, I remember being amazed observing the Crab Nebula through my telescope, thinking it funny how scientists say a nebula results when a star 'dies' in a supernova. Take the Crab Nebula. After the supernova, a pulsar remained that spins thirty times a second, the most constant source of X-rays and gamma rays in the sky — there's nothing dead about that, in my opinion.

To celebrate my move, the Gridleys invited me to dinner. Uneasily, I accepted, still nervous about Carmen. She seemed to gather her intensity from her surroundings, a swirl of energy like the contorted colours of her paintings. But I liked seeing her, even if she scared me.

In the Gridleys' living room were two white leather love seats and a matching chair around a low silver table. I found the contemporary style out of place for country living. At the window stood an easel holding Carmen's work: a pond with a fisherman done in pointillism, the tiny dots of colours spiralling like a twister, the distress in his face similar to that of the child she had painted in the orchard. More of her work decorated the walls, mostly fuzzy landscapes that often included a solitary figure I thought shouldn't be there. There were some photographs as well. In one of them, Bryan, Carmen, and others – parents or relatives, I guessed – wore Renaissance gowns and ruffs at what appeared to be a costume party.

Over dinner, Carmen spoke in a rather callous, matter-of-fact manner. 'Dad's upset about losing, but in time he'll see it's best for everybody.'

Bryan seemed depressed, saying nothing as we ate. Finally, he looked at me. 'Listen, Ed, no one blames you. Though you can understand why my father-in-law wants to live here. He loves that house. And the plan to make the barn a living space thrilled him.'

'There must be other properties for sale nearby.'

Bryan returned to his food with a tight grin. A little guilt ached in my chest.

Carmen excused herself. I thought my comment may have put her off. The sounds of a cabinet opening in the kitchen, pills rattling in a container, a faucet filling a glass, seeped into the dining area. Bryan said, 'Her father could help her out around here.'

Carmen reappeared. 'Dad doesn't belong here, Bryan.' Though it was pitch dark, for a moment she stared out the window at the pond. Bull frogs were croaking their hypnotic rhythm. 'He'd be doing too much. You keep forgetting, he's already suffered one heart attack.'

Bryan poked his fork at his plate. 'Anyway, we'll all miss Frank.'

I understood Frank was a friend to both of them, so I found it strange that Carmen didn't agree with Bryan. Instead, she acted as if she'd been rid of a pest, her glance drifting to one of her landscapes on the wall.

I shared my plan for converting the barn into an observatory. They listened politely and asked a few questions. Then I helped clear the table. I was home and in bed before ten.

I awoke to the whizz of a power drill coming from outside. I rose and peeked through the window. The barn light was on, casting a glow through its windows. Bryan, I thought, finishing a project he and Frank had left undone. But at this time of night?

The drilling went on as I dressed, but as I stepped out onto my front porch, the noise stopped and the barn light blinked off. I went back inside, grabbed a flashlight, and walked to the barn. Once there, I flipped the light switch but the light didn't come on. In the tunnel sight of the flashlight, I saw a drill plugged into the wall. On the floor were scattered rectangular plates for electrical outlets and switches, and a pile of screws. The light bulb overhead had burned out, I concluded, and Bryan had gone home.

The next afternoon, I saw him chaining up the pier that led to the new dock. He had wrapped the chain several times around two wood posts at the foot of the pier. A padlock joined the ends of the chain. He snapped the padlock shut as I walked over to him. 'Hello there, neighbour,' I said. 'More work on the deck? Thought it was done.'

'Frank watched the kids who fish and swam here. We don't care to.'

'And you think a chain will keep them out?'

'Has in the past.' Bryan's face suddenly went blank and, for the first time, I found him rather unfriendly. Nonetheless, I asked him what was going on in the barn. He had no idea what I was talking about. Either he was lying or I'd been dreaming. I considered no other possibility.

That same day, at dusk, I set up my telescope in the yard. Venus was out, the only visible object in the sky. Light from

Venus takes ten minutes to reach our eyes, so I actually viewed the past — something still there but not exactly as it was. I adjusted the settings so the telescope would point at a particular galaxy cluster. As I trudged to the house to wait until dark, I sighted a man standing at the top of the ditch about ninety feet away, the boundary of my property. I raised my hand.

'Hello there.'

The senior gentleman's black frame glasses contrasted sharply with his white hair and white suit. I walked towards him. He was crying, his shoulders jerking, tears wetting his cheeks. I said, 'Sir, what's the matter?' but he only shook his head, turned and broke into a jog, crossed the road, and lunged into an unharvested cornfield. I ran after him. Enough light remained to see between the brown stalks and ragged leaves, but I lost him.

As I returned to my telescope, my stomach knotted. I realised I'd seen him before, in the photo at the Gridleys of people in costume. He was one of them — Carmen's father, I guessed, back from the Netherlands.

I sprinted to their house. The empty driveway meant Bryan was at work. A garage light was on, the rest of the house dark. I knocked twice. No answer. Carmen must be with her father — when had he returned? — or with Bryan, I thought, or out painting. I hurried back to my telescope, packed it up, and went inside. I called the Gridleys and left a message, then called Bryan at the hospital. He was unavailable.

'Tell him it's urgent,' I said into the phone, my hand shaking.

'Sir, are you experiencing an emergency?'

'No ... I don't think so.'

I made a drink and waited two hours for someone to call. Finally I went to bed, figuring I'd hear the phone. But instead of the phone, I heard the high-pitched zinging again. I got up. The barn light was on. Mystery solved, I thought: Dr de Groesch was now a squatter, and for one more night, I decided, I would let him be.

At eight the next morning, Carmen, in her messy smock, opened her door to my knocks.

'Hi,' I said. 'Get my message?'

'Bryan was about to call you. He got your message late. He thought it could wait.'

'I called you, too.'

'I sleep deeply.'

Bryan joined us in the dining room overlooking the pond.

'Well, is your father here?' I asked Carmen.

'What?'

'Has he come back from the Netherlands?' I turned to her husband. He narrowed his eyes at me. 'I found him last night in my yard. He ran off before I could speak with him, as I told you in my message.'

'Really, Edward,' Carmen said. 'We thought you were joking.'

'No, I'm not joking. Call him. What is it, two in the afternoon there? Call. Bet I'm right.'

She placed the call; her father didn't answer, so she left a message. From Bryan's squished-up face, I couldn't tell if he was disgusted with me or mystified by what I had told him, or both. I didn't bother mentioning the drilling in the barn.

I left them and went to the barn myself, finding no one there and nothing disturbed.

Up until then, the next day was the worst of my life. Light rain fell as I drank coffee in the kitchen. My phone rang and I answered. Bryan, at the hospital, sobbed uncontrollably.

'Frank ... his car ... crashed ...'

Frank, swerving to miss a biker coming over a hill, had hit a pole. The poor man had planned to fly to New York the next day to see his daughter. Before his departure, he'd been drawn to the old house and to fish in the pond.

Shock left me silent. Finally I said I'd come to the hospital.

'No,' Bryan said. 'I'm home in an hour. Carmen knows. Please keep her company.'

A few minutes later I was in the Gridleys' living room. Carmen wore pink flannel pyjamas and a red bathrobe, cradling a box of tissues in her lap. I sat next to her on a love seat and put an arm around her, my hand grasping her shoulder. Through my own tears I said, 'Such an honourable man, Frank. We were lucky to be his friends.'

'No ... I mean yes ... but no, it's not him ...'

I tightened my grip on her shoulder. She turned to me, her face colourless except for her bloodshot eyes. Her next words hit me so hard, for an instant my grief disappeared.

'My father passed away. A stroke.' She drove her head into my shoulder, crying and speaking at the same time. 'His neighbour just called. They found him in his apartment ... he'd been dead more than a day.'

In the span of fifteen minutes I'd learned that two people I knew were deceased. A sad numbness consumed me. After Bryan was back, I walked home. In the far corner of the orchard I paused to gaze upon the grand house Father had built. Was the timing of the two deaths just a coincidence? The question bothered me then; even more so now.

The Gridleys weren't able to attend Frank's funeral. They had boarded a plane for the Netherlands. Before he left, Bryan gave me more details about the accident. Frank was driving sixty miles an hour without wearing his seat belt. He went through the windshield, crushing his right cheekbone and jaw. He died of a heart attack.

I went alone to the funeral. His daughters wanted an open casket, a challenge given Frank's half-collapsed face. When I viewed him, he looked quite natural, though the cadaver cream filling his right cheek made it puffy and paler than the left. They buried him next to his son in Hudson's cemetery. Carved into Erik's headstone were two fishing poles forming an X with dangling lines, bobbers, and hooks. In similar fashion, Frank's headstone displayed a hammer and screwdriver that crossed, reminding me of all the work he put into the house. In that moment, I felt a duty to be a good steward to Windy Acres, and like Frank, a faithful friend.

I decided I was mistaken about Carmen's father. Just because Dr de Groesch didn't take her call did not mean he wasn't in Haarlem at the time I thought I saw him in my yard. Doppelgangers really exist, I assured myself. I had not thought to ask her if he ever returned her phone call. I saw no reason to ask her now.

November evenings are too cold to observe stars outdoors. The first night after the Gridleys returned, I set up my telescope upstairs in front of a window facing east. I pointed it at Saturn, anxious to see Titan. Saturn's largest moon is one of those gorgeous places where nothing lives; nothing known to science, that is. Around ten, just as my telescope found Titan's orange haze, the sharp zinging noise started again. Peering out another window, I wasn't surprised to see the barn light on. My phone rang. This time, Carmen.

'Edward, do you hear? Somebody's in the barn.'

'Bryan, right?'

'No, he's at the hospital.'

She heard the drilling too. Frightened, she had already called the Hudson police. She asked me to come over. I got a flashlight and my coat. When I arrived, she looked shaken, hugging herself with her arms. The police were supposed to be there within an hour. They instructed her to stay indoors.

While she made gin cocktails, I studied her painting of the pond. She had altered the fisherman. His face, enlarged out of proportion with the rest of the swirling scene, was more twisted and disfigured than before, crying for attention. She served the cocktails by the window overlooking the barn. A yellow glow enveloped the building. As power tools roared on and off, Carmen revealed she was thinking about leaving Bryan. 'I want to move, try something new, but he won't hear of it.'

I felt a pang of loss, which told me perhaps she, more than anything, was now the reason I was at Windy Acres.

After a second cocktail she called the police again. They told her to be patient.

She went on about how moody Bryan had become, how she thought he was reliving the pain of losing his own father as a boy. 'Bryan and Frank were like this.' She pressed two fingers together and raised them. 'And he couldn't save Frank's life. Frank was driving here when his car crashed, and Bryan wanted to ...'

'Go on. Bryan wanted to do what?'

She stared into her glass. 'He wanted to ask Frank's family to bury him here. He had even picked a spot and ...'

She raised her glass and drank, then lowered it and wrapped her hands around the glass.

'And?'

'Bryan suggested we bring dad back, too. I told him he was insane.'

I didn't disagree with her.

Twenty more minutes passed and Bryan still wasn't home. Carmen called him, heard the ring of his phone, and found it in the living room. He seemed to have forgotten it. All the while, the whirling outside went on.

'All right, enough,' I said, gesturing at the window with my glass. 'I'm checking out the barn.'

'No, Edward. We're supposed to stay here.'

'Look. Thieves would be gone by now. Keep the doors locked.'

She went to the other window, the one facing the pond, studying the darkness before swinging back to me.

'No, I won't be left alone.'

'What do you mean?'

'I'm coming with you.'

She went to a drawer, threw it open, and jerked out a flashlight. I gave in to her. We downed our drinks, put on our coats, and plunged into the night each holding a flashlight. Our steps grew shorter the closer we got to the barn, and were baby steps by the time we reached the door. Things suddenly fell quiet. The light remained on. Nodding at Carmen's flashlight, I said, 'We won't need these,' and we clicked them off.

As soon as I turned the knob and opened the door, the light went out. We clicked our flashlights back on and we both gasped. At the table before us sat three people, illuminated in our beams. Frank Speery smiled unevenly with a lopsided cheek. To his left sat a kid with a purplish face, wearing a baseball cap that tilted and revealed a bruise above his blackened right eye. The bottom half of his face was a violet hue, his expression one of sad astonishment. Erik. On Frank's other side was Dr de Groesch. Carmen gurgled from the back of her throat, struggling to say 'Dad,' as the loud whizzing of a drill started again. Exactly where it came from I couldn't tell, but it was deafening.

The doctor wore the same white suit and was crying, his tears dropping onto the table without making a puddle. I raised the shaky beam of my flashlight at the open door leading to the hay shed. The light revealed a torso from the waist down, tan cowboy boots dangling a yard above the floor.

Carmen's scream blasted to my left for ten seconds, and I reflexively put a hand over my left ear. Still screaming, she ran to Bryan. Frank, Erik, and Dr de Groesch all rose and stepped into her path. She stopped and turned around to me, her mouth agape. I braced for another scream, which didn't come. Instead she fled past me, out the barn, the beam of her flashlight bouncing in every direction.

I faced the three figures. They glowed like animations in black outer space. I charged them, swinging my flashlight like a club so I could get to Bryan. It made no impact, simply passed through them. I dropped the flashlight and hugged and lifted Bryan's legs to create slack in the rope. I kept supporting him as I faced the open door and shuddered. They were seated again, and I saw them from behind. The back of Frank's head was shaved, a large square missing from his lower skull, a fluffy material sticking out, as if somebody had crammed a pillow into the cavity. Then all of them stood again, drifted to me and put their hands on my arms, trying to push me away from Bryan. If he wasn't dead yet that's clearly what they wanted, but I felt nothing touching me and, even in my terror, I didn't budge. The whirling buzz was vibrating my teeth. Suddenly I heard the siren of the police.

Nobody except me believes this, but looking back, I'm sure the noise in my ear is the sound of the spirits trying to use the power tools. When I covered my left ear, the horrific noise filled my other ear and stayed there. Yes, I know. The doctors found nothing in the ear canal or cochlea, no abnormality. Nothing's trapped in there. Nonetheless, when Bryan's fingers spread themselves over my face, I felt them locking up the noise. Raising him had loosened the noose, allowing him to breathe and regain consciousness. His boots came to rest on my back, his hands released my face, and he twisted off the noose. We both tumbled to the dirt.

The light came on. The others were gone. Bryan slowly picked himself up, rubbing his neck, then caught sight of me. He turned and ran. I never saw him or Carmen again. In shock, I stayed frozen in the light, waiting for the police. Hammers, boxes of nails and screws, a power jigsaw, and three power drills were spread out on the table along with building plans. Nothing had moved since the last time I'd been there.

Yesterday, I checked in with my agent, who told me the new owners of the house had hired a crew to work on the barn.

'So nothing unusual?' I asked.

'How do you mean?'

'Never mind. What are they doing to the barn?'

'Turning it into a guest house.'

'How many bedrooms?'

'Three.'

'Good move.'

My agent is supposed to tell me when the barn is finished, which is my best hope for silence. Once the tools are put away everyone ought to be happy, including me. I've told my therapist let's wait and see if I'm right before contacting any more doctors. In the meantime, I'll cope with the help of planets and stars. Tonight in alignment are Jupiter, Venus, and Mars. Actually, they're aligned right now. You just can't notice them until dark.

Ghosts, of course, have never been the only thing to inspire fear in our lives. Take for instance the danger from a burglar on the prowl in your neighbourhood, or the stress of keeping your family safe and provided for in straitened circumstances and a broken housing market. Sharon in Jerry Ibbotson's story does take all these things, and more besides...

The Intruder

Jerry Ibbotson

'The bathroom is pretty small.'

The letting agent stood in the doorway while Sharon peered past her at the lime green tiles speckled with black mould. The white bathtub and plastic shower curtain were both stained with orange streaks. A single green toothbrush had been abandoned in a cup on the windowsill, bristles akimbo. There was a cabinet on the wall above the toilet with a handprint splashed across the mirrored door. Everything smelled of bleach.

'I don't need much more,' Sharon said. The agent coughed and moved away to the main bedroom. A double bed: four pillows in place, a duvet rolled up in the middle of the mattress. Two small chests of drawers. A large built-in wardrobe with white laminate doors. Floral curtains at the window. There wasn't much more to see.

'I'll take it.'

The agent stared in disbelief, no longer even trying to hide her surprise and disgust at Sharon's low standards. There was even a quiet sigh as she reached into her shoulder bag and produced the paperwork.

As Sharon got to the car she looked back at the late-sixties semi, set in a small square of similar looking houses. The gutter above the front bedroom window bowed in the middle and there were three loose roof tiles. The paintwork was dull and faded. This house had seen better days.

You'll do.

The agent was locking up the front door. She spotted Sharon. There was a shake of the head. She might not even have been aware of it but she definitely shook her head.

Oh fuck you.

'Where's my box load of games?' Sam called from downstairs.

'By the front window.'

She went back to emptying a suitcase full of clothes. Each item shouted its history at her as she unfolded it.

Long sleeve top. Bought in the Lake District three years ago. The same day we ate fish and chips in the car.

She dropped it in a drawer.

'I've looked there.'

'Look harder.'

Sharon stood by the bed and waited. One, two, three...

'Got it! It was by the window.'

Jeans with a hole in the knee. Bought in the sales two years ago. We'd been to the cinema in the morning. Can't even remember the film.

They went in the wardrobe.

'Mum! The bed's wobbly.' Thomas's voice came through the wall.

She put the clothes sorting on hold and went into the next room to tighten some screws. After a minute the doorbell rang.

'You carry on,' she said, handing Thomas the Allen key. He looked at it in surprise. 'Righty tightey, lefty loosey,' she said and went downstairs.

There was a woman at the door. Late sixties. White hair and quite a lot of make-up.

She introduced herself as Maureen from two doors down. 'I just wanted to say hello and see if you needed anything.'

'We're just unpacking at the moment, but I think we'll be alright.'

Maureen held her hands close to her chest, her knuckles almost as white as her hair. 'Well that's good. But if there are any problems...'

A husband dead from cancer maybe? Or having no money and two teenagers to raise?

'Problems?'

Maureen's mouth moved strangely. It was trying to form words but nothing was coming out.

Does she know she's doing that?

Eventually she said, 'Well, anything at all,' before stepping away from the door and saying goodbye. Sharon closed the door in a controlled manner. She didn't want it to slam and risk pissing off her neighbours on day one, but she wanted to get back upstairs. In the end it slammed anyway.

An hour later, with all beds fully tightened, there was more noise from the front door. A newspaper was being pushed through the narrow letterbox, wiggling and twisting from left to right as it came through. She opened the door to find a boy of about fourteen staring at his now-empty fingers.

'Thought I'd save you the bother,' she said.

The teenager looked from his hand to her and back. His fingers were shaking. He backed away and hurried to the bicycle that lay on the lawn. One foot flicked a pedal round and he was off. He looked back once, a glance that lasted just long enough for Sharon to see the look in his eyes.

What's he afraid of? I don't bite. Much.

She glanced down at the paper, to a headline about a break-in, then closed the door and went back to the unpacking.

'Mum, what does "aggravated" mean?'

'Pretty much how I feel most days. Why?'

Tom appeared in the kitchen holding his phone. 'They were talking at school about this.' He held the phone out to her. 'Something called aggravated burglary. It's happened twice down the road.'

She reached out and steadied Tom's hand, straining to read the online article he was shoving in her face.

People hunting attacker... aggravated burglary on local couple... serious injuries... similar case two weeks ago...

'That's nice. And what were they saying about it at school?' She let go of her son's wrist.

'Just that he beats people up in their own homes.'

'Could be a she?'

'No Mum.' Tom's voice was full of withering disapproval. 'It's got to be a bloke. It's always a bloke.'

'Are you proud of that fact?'

He gave her one of his idiot looks. 'Of course not. I'm just saying. It'll be a bloke.' Then he went back to staring at his phone.

Just what I need, some nut-job on the prowl.

Another knock at the door. A woman in her thirties. Angry lines on her face.

Does everyone round here look like that? Is it a thing?

'Are you the one who's just moved in?'

'I am. Yes. And you are?'

'Emma Pearson. I lived here before.'

The name rang a bell. 'Oh. I think I've got some of your post. Let me fetch it.'

She went to move indoors but the woman reached out and put one hand on the door frame. It was enough to root Sharon to the spot. 'No, I don't want my post. I just need to talk about the house.'

'Do you want to come in?' Sharon wanted to pull the words back in, the second they left her lips.

Why did I say that? The woman's wired.

She needn't have worried. 'No. I don't want to come inside. Not there. That's the thing. The house isn't healthy.'

'Excuse me?'

'It's not a good place to live. They know that.'

'Who knows that? And what is "that"?'

The hand on the door was drawn away.

'The letting agency. They know I had problems here and I thought they weren't going to rent it out again. At least until they'd been sorted.'

'What kind of problems?'

Thomas appeared, dropping off the last few stairs into the hallway and bouncing away towards the kitchen. The sight of him made the woman at the door even more agitated.

'You've got kids? And they let you in there with kids?'

She's scaring me now.

'Look, I'm sorry but I'm very busy. I'd love to chat but I've got things to do. Let me just fetch that post for you.'

This time a foot came out and pressed against the bottom of the door.

'Fuck my post. Just get out of this house. It's a bad place.'

Sharon snapped. 'Oh fuck off yourself.' She kicked the foot away and slammed the door shut.

Her visitor wasn't giving up, even with a door between them. 'I'm trying to help you,' she said. The anger had gone. She sounded hurt. Desperate.

'I don't need help,' Sharon said through the woodwork.

Don't encourage her. Back away.

She went into the kitchen, where Thomas was helping himself to the contents of the fridge. It was only as she was holding a glass under the cold tap that she realised how much her hands were shaking.

'Are you okay, Mum?' Thomas asked. Then, 'Why is there a woman crying outside our front door?'

Emma Pearson was still there. Her sobs were muffled by the front door, but that just made them sound even more pathetic.

'Just ignore her,' Sharon said, gripping the glass to ease the tremors in her fingers. 'She'll go away in a minute.'

Three days in, and the first experience. Sharon was getting ready to go to bed. The boys were already upstairs. She went round switching off lights.

Why am I the only one to do this?

The hall light first. Then the kitchen. She moved into the lounge. That was when she felt it. The sense that someone had just left the room. She went back into the hall and called upstairs.

'Boys? Are you both in bed?'

'I'm watching something,' Sam said, over the sound of music.

'Tom?' There was no answer. 'Thomas?'

She climbed the stairs and gently pushed at his door. His lamp was off but the glow from the landing light reached into the room. She could see him fast asleep on his bed. His mouth was wide open and a thread of dribble ran from his lip.

She repeated her check of the downstairs lights. Hall first, then straight to the lounge. Again, the second she walked in, there was the feeling that someone had just left. There was a weight to the air. A break in the usual stillness of an empty room. She scanned the room for anything out of the ordinary. The windows were all closed.

Someone had just been in here. She was sure of it.

She retreated upstairs, flicking the hall light back on as she went. It took her a few minutes for the feeling to pass.

Broad daylight this time. She walked into the lounge after waving the kids off to school. Her bag was on the coffee table and she went to pick it up and head out to work. Halfway across the carpet it hit. There was somebody there with her. She looked around the room. A reflex. Checking who it was.

No one, dummy. The house is empty.

But it wasn't empty. Her brain told her that someone was in the lounge alongside her. It was as simple as that. Like knowing there was a glass of flat coke on the bookcase, left over from the night before.

But the glass really was there. She could see it. The person was not.

Because I can't see them.

But they were there. Her brain said so. It screamed so.

There was a sofa and two chairs. Her bag was on the table. The glass was on the bookcase. And...

Someone is in the room with me. They are here.

She stood for a moment and scanned the room. Left to right and back again. No one. Nothing. She was alone in the house.

No. No I am not.

She closed her eyes, scrunching them tight and counting to ten. She only lasted until eight before opening them again.

Nothing. Nothing at all.

The voice that had been screaming at her was now just a murmur. She grabbed her bag and left.

'Have you noticed anything odd about the place?'

Tom peered up from his phone. 'What sort of odd?'

'Just Odd odd. Anything at all?' Sharon looked away and focused on stirring the pasta sauce on the cooker. She didn't want to spook him.

'Simon at school reckons that burglar guy's an escaped psycho. His brother told him. Is that what you mean?'

'Not really.' She stirred the sauce. This was not going well. 'But I'm sure it's just a burglar. Nothing more than that. And I meant something else entirely.'

Tom gave her one of his looks. She could see him out of the corner of her eye. There was nothing worse than the withering disdain of a teenager. She felt even more stupid now.

'But if you do notice anything odd, tell me.'

There was another look. She felt the burn of her son's disapproval, even as she stared into the pan of bubbling sauce. He sighed and left the kitchen.

The next few days were all about work and domestic duties. Trying to keep on top of stuff at the office while juggling two separate parents' evenings, a school concert, and an Everest of washing. The school events were difficult. Every other kid had two parents with them. She was there alone. It was highly likely no one even noticed her but she imagined them pitying her.

Fuck 'em. Fuck 'em all.

The weekend finally arrived and she was determined not to leave the house, to spend forty-eight solid hours indoors. Saturday morning was easy. She got up early to make tea and toast, to put a load of washing on and to clear some dishes. Then she went back to bed.

Thomas made his own breakfast and left the house to play football with his friends. Sam was in his room, playing with his phone. She closed her eyes and dozed for a while. When she woke up and reached for her tea it was cold.

Her tiredness fought a battle with the desire for another brew. She considered sending the boy downstairs to make her a drink but decided against it.

That's tantamount to slavery. He'll tell his teacher or ring Childline.

Instead, she swung herself out of bed and went down to the kitchen. The kettle was just coming to the boil when she felt it. The sensation that someone was in the living room. Even through a solid wall she could tell that someone was in there. A disturbance in the air. A change to the hum of the house. Something shifted in the universe around her and she knew the room next door was occupied.

The kettle was boiling, rattling and hissing as it reached a climax. The sounds of Sam's game were trickling down from his room. But someone was in the lounge. She went through.

A quick scan. Left to right and back. Always left to right. Never right to left. Not that it mattered.

Nothing.

Her eyes and ears told her there was no one there. But her brain said something else. Soaking up information from some other source, it told her that someone was in the room. Sitting on the sofa.

There was no sign of any disturbance. No impression on the cushion beyond the usual creases and dents left by two teenage boys. But someone was sitting there. They had their hands on their knees and were looking towards the television.

They are here. Now. Right here.

There was no part of her that understood what was happening, what was in the room with her. She had nothing to compare it to, no previous experience to act as a baseline. Nothing Sharon had ever seen, or heard or touched could help her comprehend it. And the sense of simply not knowing, not understanding, created a primeval reaction.

Fear.

The emptiness, the void in her knowledge, was what terrified her. It flooded through her veins like adrenaline. Her fingers trembled. Her knees became weak. She felt she was about to buckle and fold. Something inside her was being drawn out, the warmth escaping from her body in a rush.

I don't understand this.

She found her voice and called out.

'Sam?'

There was silence. Then a muffled reply. 'Yeah?'

'Sam...' If she said his name enough times he'd eventually be drawn downstairs out of annoyance and curiosity. Then he'd come in and glare at her. He'd give her one of those looks that would break the spell. He'd shake his head at his mad mother and she'd laugh it off.

'Sam...'

He was already halfway down the stairs. Then he was in the room. He looked at her and she braced herself for the disapproval and pubescent scorn. Happy to accept the silent shake of his head.

But he just stopped. His eyes were no longer on her. They were on the sofa. His lips moved but he didn't say a word. He just stared at that spot, his brain sprinting to catch up with hers. Her little boy was afraid.

'Yes.' That was all she could manage. She so wished she'd left him upstairs now and dealt with this herself. He was meant to dismiss this, not validate it.

Her hand reached out and took his.

'What is it?' he said, pulling himself into her.

'I don't know.' Then she laughed. 'That's an understatement. I really don't have a fucking clue...'

'Mum, you swore.'

After a moment, they managed to detach themselves from each other and draw back from the room. They went up and sat on Sam's bed and talked.

'Is it a ghost, Mum? Is there a ghost in this house?'

'On our sofa? Possibly.'

'But they don't exist, do they?'

'I don't know. I'm sorry.' She took his hand again. 'I don't have an answer. To be honest, I'm not even sure I know my own name right now.'

'It's Sharon, Mum.'

She didn't know if he was being funny or oddly literal. She laughed anyway.

Then he said, 'Is it Dad?'

This time she thought before answering. 'If it is a ghost, then I don't think it is Dad.'

'Why not?'

She thought of the frightened, ranting woman at her front door. She'd been afraid of something in the house. But there was no point in scaring her son any more than he was already. 'I just do. We'd have seen him before, wouldn't we?'

The boy thought on this. She could see his brain whirring behind his eyes.

His beautiful brown eyes. Just like his father's.

Maybe it is Michael. Come back to haunt me. From the sofa.

'Do you think it wants to hurt us?' The boy had finished his thinking and the brown eyes were narrowed and pin-sharp.

It was enough to raise her from the bed.

Michael would never let anyone hurt them. He'd do whatever it took.

She went back to the lounge and shut the door behind her. The sense of something being in the room was as strong as before. It was still there on the sofa, enjoying a peaceful sit-down in front of the telly. Whatever this thing was, it seemed in no rush to move.

'I don't know what you are.' There was a shake in her voice which she forced herself to throw off. 'But I've got a message for you.' She inched towards the sofa. 'Stay away from my boys. Don't you dare fuck with them.'

She was standing in front of it and could sense it considering her. It was listening to her and thinking.

'Scaring me is one thing. I've been scared before. Watch someone die and you'll know fear. But do not fuck with them. Not ever.'

It was drawing breath. She knew it was. Then it exhaled.

Her knees went first. She buckled and fell to the carpet. Pain washed over her like a breaking wave, knocking the air from her lungs. One hand reached out and grabbed at the sofa for balance.

It's like ice. So cold.

She slid further, her face hitting the floor. There was a voice in her head and it wasn't hers.

I have nowhere else to go.

They didn't say that much about what had happened. Thomas came back from football and wondered why Sharon was in the kitchen nursing a bloody nose. They did their best to explain it all to him without sounding mad. It was difficult. He said he believed them but she wasn't sure if he meant it.

But after that they skipped around the subject. The lounge wasn't strictly out of bounds but no one went in there for more than a few seconds at a time. The sofa, however, had an exclusion zone of at least a metre.

This went on for four days. On day five, Sharon had waved the boys off and was doing some hasty accounts on the back of an envelope. They had just enough money to get to the end of the month. She checked the time: five minutes past the point when she should have been at the bus stop.

Bollocks.

Her coat went on. Then she checked for change in her purse. Fifty pence short. She knew where there were some more coins. On the arm of the sofa. She went to the lounge door and looked in. Everything seemed fine. Not a hair out of place. But the second she stepped in, she knew. It was in there with her. Or she was in there with it. Whichever came first.

She withdrew. The thumping in her chest was so powerful it pulsated all the way up to her throat. She was afraid of everything. Of not knowing what this was. Of the possibilities of what it might be. Of feeling more pain and cold.

She looked down at the scrunched-up envelope in her hand. Her life and the boys' happiness laid out in a list of income versus expenditure.

Fuck it.

She returned to the kitchen, grabbed a pen and returned to the lounge. This time she went to the coffee table, laid the envelope down and wrote. Then she dropped the pen, snatched up the coins from the sofa and left the house.

You have nowhere else to go? Well neither do we.

It was an odd teatime. She bought fish and chips with scraps and mushy peas and even buttered some bread to go with it. The boys were keen to get stuck in, but then she said, 'We're eating in there,' and nodded through the kitchen wall. They looked horrified.

'Joking yeah?' Thomas said. Sam didn't speak.

'No. We're eating in front of the telly. It's our home and we'll go where the f— where we damn well like.' Then she marched through and sat at the other end of the sofa. The end that wasn't occupied.

She turned the television on and flicked to a channel showing old sitcoms. 'Come and watch this. It was one of your dad's favourites.'

There was a pause, just long enough for her to cut off a chunk of battered haddock and put it in her mouth. Then Sam appeared at the door. She said nothing, keeping her gaze on the telly and her mouth occupied with the fish. The boy gradually moved into the room, his gaze flicking from the screen to the sofa and back. He made it to one of the armchairs and dropped down. Now his attention settled entirely on the sitcom. He started on the fish and chips and even laughed at one of the jokes.

It took his brother another couple of minutes to follow suit. They heard him clattering about in the kitchen for a while, for no obvious reason. Then he came into the lounge with his head down and his hands gripping the plate. He went straight to the other chair, sat down and began eating. It took another minute for his legs to stop shaking but eventually he relaxed into his seat.

All three of them were aware that the far end of the sofa had someone on it. They were picking that up loud and clear. But they did their best to ignore it and eat their tea. No one spoke to begin with, the only sound being the canned laughter from the TV. But eventually Sharon said, 'So, how was school?' and, to her surprise, the boys answered. They actually spoke to her and told her about who had done what to whom and why that day. They explained in gory detail about the fight at lunchtime and relished telling her about which couple had split up because one of them had been caught with someone else's brother. Or sister. She got lost somewhere on that one.

They never stopped being aware of the presence in the room. They always had that feeling of someone else being there with them. But it slipped from the foreground to the background. And as their brains stopped dwelling on it, the fear in them went away. They didn't know exactly when it happened but they each realised that they no longer had that inside them anymore.

'Should we do something about that space?' Sam said eventually. 'Maybe mark it in some way, in case someone else comes round?'

Sharon thought on this. Then she left the room for a minute, returning with an old tartan rug from the cupboard on the landing. 'Let's try this. It looks a bit like a dog blanket. People might think a dog sits there.'

'But we don't have a dog,' Sam said. There were the beginnings of a look.

'Really? That's what you take from this?' his brother said.

Sharon approached the other end of the sofa, the rug held out in front like a fire blanket. She laid it down gently on the seat and spread it flat, feeling the chill from the cushion. Bracing herself for a reaction, she tucked it neatly around the edges and backed away. There was no pain. No inner voice screaming at her.

Then they all went back to watching the telly.

'Boys, lights out. And that means phones too.' Sharon waited at the foot of the stairs for a response. The light under Sam's door flicked off but Thomas's remained stubbornly on. 'I want you both settled before I come up,' she said, before retreating to the lounge to finish her tea.

The paperboy had been that evening, looking as scared as ever, and he'd shoved the local free weekly through the letterbox. She scanned the front page: dominated by crime and violence.

We could tell you a story worth printing.

Not that anyone would believe them.

She drained the tea, dumped the mug in the sink and headed to bed. Thomas's light was finally off and her own followed suit within minutes.

It was like being woken by the rumble of an earthquake. Not strictly a sound but the sensation of energy being released. Sharon was upright in bed just as Sam appeared in her room. 'Mum, what was that?'

'No idea.' She flicked the lamp on her bedside table but nothing happened. Sam hit the switch on the wall. Ditto.

Thomas was there too. The boys came into the room, their forms silhouetted by the glow of the street light beyond the window. They made for her bed.

Then they felt it. The three of them knew there was movement downstairs. The air in the lounge was shifting and parting.

'Oh my god, it's angry,' Sam said. 'I can feel how angry it is.' He started to cry.

'Why is it angry?' Thomas was gripping the bed. 'Is it coming to get us?'

Sharon moved to the bedroom door and kicked it shut with her bare feet. Then she ran back to the bed and drew her sons close.

'I don't know, boys. I don't know.'

That's the problem. I never fucking know anything.

They huddled together, the boys resting on her shoulders. She stroked their hair and braced herself.

Then there was a bang. An actual one. Not a sixth-sense tremor but a physical crash. And another. The sound of glass breaking and the most godawful noise she'd ever heard: a piercing scream of pain and terror.

They felt another movement in the air. Hard and fast, like a punch being thrown. Then there was the sound of more glass breaking and a second cry. The noises were coming from outside now. Whimpering and the sound of footsteps moving away.

They stayed together on the bed, eyes closed.

Sharon had no idea what time it was, but eventually there were more voices outside. Then a knock at the door. She stayed where she was, still stroking the boys' hair. Another knock and then,

'Hello?' A woman was calling from outside the house. 'Hello, is there anyone in?'

Sharon untangled herself from the boys and went to the bedroom door. She edged down the stairs, pressing her body to the wall. She flicked the latch on the front door and was greeted by a tunnel of light from a torch.

'I'm a police officer. We think you should come with us...'

'Gary Taylor says the bloke's in a mad house.' Sam was wide-eyed and grinning.

'They don't call them mad houses,' Thomas said witheringly. 'But I heard he can't even talk properly. And he broke both arms and a leg.'

'Do people at school have nothing better to talk about?' Sharon said.

The boys looked at each other and back to her.

'No,' they said.

'Well I can tell you direct that he's not in a mad house but he is in hospital. And yes, he did break quite a few bones falling through our window.'

'Falling. Right. Yeah.' Tom was grinning now.

'Yes, Thomas. That is what the police say happened. None of us is strong enough to have thrown him. They say he was on something when he committed all those burglaries and that's why he had some kind of fit in our front room.'

'Of course, Mum.' Sam was revving up for the mother of all looks.

They took their plates into the lounge. Another chippie tea in front of the telly. Now in a house with a boarded-up window.

I win at parenting. I so do.

The TV went on and the boys started laughing. Sharon wasn't sure, but she thought she heard a voice. It was hard to tell over the canned laughter but she was pretty sure she heard it.

We've nowhere else to go. None of us.

*It could be argued that the following story is more science fiction
than ghost story, but tales of the supernatural have often sought
to explain the workings behind a haunting. Some of these
explanations are more convincing, more grounded in science,
than others; in the end, a ghost in a machine is still a ghost.*

The Dead Lie Dreaming

Seth Marlin

The first time I was allowed to see my sister, she had been dead for
nearly a year. I would have been twelve at the time, still just a girl,
the same age as my own daughter now. I remember riding with my
father out to the shrine; it was an hour's drive across the city, on
a campus of green lawns and vast reflecting pools. We signed in at
the front desk and I remember taking in the décor: high-ceilinged,
restful, almost clinical.

We were led through bright corridors. Out the windows we
could see the skylit crypts, see the stacks where the rows of peaceful
dead lay dreaming. I remember the hum of air, the echo of our
footsteps on the floors. We were led into a room and made to sit
in chairs — this would have been almost thirty years ago, when the
technology was bulkier, more primitive. The lights were low and I
remember hearing music, though perhaps music is not quite the
correct word.

'Try and relax,' said one of the techs. 'Just close your eyes and breathe.' They placed headphones over my ears, and when they did the sound grew louder, invaded my skull, turned the world strange upon alien fulcrums.

I opened my eyes and found myself standing beside my father. We were in a park not far from where I grew up. It was nighttime, and though it was summer outside in the real world, it was snowing wherever my sister was now.

'Mira?' my father said. 'Mira, are you here?' We walked then among the pines, down along the lamplit paths. Eventually we rounded a bend and there, standing in a circle of light, was my sister. She had her hands in the pockets of her sweater, staring at her feet as if thinking. She looked up when she heard us coming, grinned at my father, as if exasperated. 'I was coming home in just a minute,' she said.

'I know.' He smiled then, smiled in a way that I have never seen him smile in real life. 'We were out for a walk is all. Sweetie, what is this, what are you wearing? Don't you want a better coat? Aren't you cold?'

She shook her head. My sister, I have long since realised, is never cold. She shrugged at any rate, saw me instead and frowned. 'Cleo?' she asked. 'What's wrong?'

I didn't respond. The last time I had seen her, the casket was already being loaded into the back of the hearse. I'd had nightmares that whole week afterward of her corpse lying pale and disfigured upon a slab somewhere. I'd imagined her in the treatment baths out at the shrine, cocooned in webs of carbon filament. Meanwhile in the render she smiled and a knot came up in my throat; my father put his hand on my arm, said to me very gently 'Cleo,' and the next thing I knew I was crying. I cried. I disregarded his warnings, went up and embraced my sister and I cried. I remembered the warmth of her arms, how she smelled like the vanilla lotion she used to wear. I held her and I sobbed, told her how much we'd missed her, and this was when she stiffened and pulled away. 'Missed me?' she said. She looked as though she didn't understand. She glanced at my father, smiled as if seeking some explanation in his gaze. When none came she turned to me again, shook her head as if dismissing some unpleasant thought. 'I missed you too,' she said. 'Come here. Come into the light. Let me look at you.'

My sister is seventeen years old. Her name is Miranda, though she prefers when people call her Mir or Mira or Miri. In the dream-spaces of the render, she has dark hair and eyes of a deep, unnatural blue — I say unnatural because they never looked that way in life. They are the blue now of lapis lazuli, etched with gold like the graphene fibres that have leached away her memories, ossified her bones. I was told once that this eye colouring was a quirk of the render, a glitch that some future update would one day address. It was never explained to me how, nor what exactly made this feature a glitch. Regardless, it has been over twenty-seven years. The colour of her eyes has not changed.

My sister is beautiful. She will always be beautiful.

My sister has been seventeen for nearly three decades now. She died when I was eleven, killed by a drunk-driver one night in early February. My father was with her the night that it happened, had in fact been picking her up from high-school play practice. Even now, sitting in the nursing home, one can see on him the scar of her departure: a ragged fold, stretching from one corner of his mouth, up his cheek. In some lights it looks as though he is smiling; in others, as though his face were still twisted by grief. When he paid to have my sister enshrined, my mother could not take it and so she left him, left us both. Divorce is supposed to be a sin, I know, but I suppose she considered what we had done an even greater sin. An abomination.

The logic of enshrinement is simple: the body dies, the nerves and neurons oxidise, but the data within is still viable. It can be recovered. Where in the past we flooded corpses with formaldehyde, now we embalm them in nanofluids, in baths of solvents and liquid carbon and light metals. We enshrine the bodies of those we love, allow gardens of circuitry to tunnel inside their flesh, and with the information that is extracted we can commune, can interface with our loved ones long after they have gone. I think now of our ancestors, lighting their incenses before painted altars. Is this what they so desperately sought? I think of Mass as a child, standing with my mother and reciting the Nicene Creed. *We acknowledge one baptism for the forgiveness of sins; we look for the resurrection of the dead, and for the life of the world to come.* I wonder now: where is that world? Does it lie in our loved ones' dreams, or in our own? We always expected that conquering death would answer all our questions. Instead, we find only new ones.

I read an article last week on my tablet, about a suicide that had been circulating in the news. It concerned a young woman, twenty years old, who climbed a high balcony ledge, inserted a pair of earbuds, opened her arms and then tumbled into the downtown traffic below. Witnesses say her hair caught the light as she fell, that it fluttered in the wind until the moment she struck the pavement. When the onlookers got to her body they found her still wearing the earbuds, clutching a receiver in the bloody wet ball of her fist. We may never know whose frequency she was listening to, but we all know what she was seeking. It can be so easy, I think, to be seduced by the dreams of the dead: to feel more alive, more real in their world than in our own. She must have thought she was leaving us all behind, leaving her pain to go and be with the ones that she loved. Would that it worked that way. When I finished reading I went out with my coffee, sipped and stared and stood on my porch, listening to the wind chimes. It was a bright cool morning on my residential street. The leaves were very green. They whispered gentle rumours overhead.

Later I went to visit my sister. My lesson plans and my writing were done for the day, so I went upstairs, lay down and took out the receiver I keep in my nightstand. I inserted the earbuds and adjusted the volume, listened to that strange sweet music again. I found my sister alone in the park, in daylight. She lay in the grass picking dandelions, smiled at my approach as though nothing were any different. Afterward I woke up and went downstairs. The sun had moved in the sky, and I remember feeling tired. I heard dinnerware clattering, came into the kitchen to find my daughter Rheya putting away the dishes. She is twelve now, and so very tall for her age. Her shoes were kicked off by the door. On the stovetop, a covered skillet was simmering.

'Stroganoff,' she said. 'I tried to keep it warm.'

I went to see my father in the nursing home recently. His condition is growing worse. He spends nearly all his time in bed now, sleeps for most of the day, and can no longer be bothered with actions like bathing or feeding himself. His attentions drift during conversation: to an image of a hummingbird on the television, to a scuff on the tiled floor, a speck of dust, dancing, in the light from the window. He told me a rambling anecdote about my mother during our visit, as though they were only just recently engaged. Twice he called me by my sister's name. Twice. He did not address me by my own name even once.

Afterward, I spoke with his doctor, a soft balding man in his forties. He advised me that it could be less than a year now, invited me to talk with him at length about options. How I hate that word. The first time I heard it was in the office of another doctor, a fertility specialist, near the end of my wasted twenties. I remember that doctor's hands also, how they rubbed together as he talked about things like sequencing alternatives and confidential donors. I remember cutting him off, saying 'I already know what I want.' I remember pushing the envelope across his desk, the way he opened it, the way he peered inside at its contents. The way his eyes grew wide with understanding, then with terrible pity. Meanwhile back in the present my father's physician advised me to be realistic. He told me how, given the rare and degenerative nature of my father's dementia, he would not be a fit candidate for enshrinement. 'You'll need to move on,' he said. 'These things do happen. The science just isn't quite there yet. I'm sorry.'

Several days ago, I received a call from my daughter's school. She was in detention, I was told, and could I please come by for a word? The principal was waiting when I arrived, and at her insistence we went back to her office. Together we watched a recording dance in the air above her desk: a meeting in the school auditorium, a memorial for a girl who had recently died. Melissa was her name, I recalled, and she had been Rheya's friend at school. Her best friend. She had drowned while on a hiking trip with her family, fallen into a river high with summer floods. They found her body in a tangle of reeds, some six miles from where they had lost her. In the memorial clip the principal showed, there was no audio, only a scene of flowers and a podium atop a stage. In the background, a larger-than-life photo of Melissa herself. Another girl was speaking into a microphone, sniffling and wiping her cheeks, when the camera panned, and then there was Rheya, stomping up the stairs from stage left. She grabbed the microphone away, knocked over the flowers, and began shouting at the rest of the audience. When the point had been made the principal tapped her desk and the image froze suspended. I kept on looking: in my daughter's dark hair, her blue eyes, I saw only my sister. The principal smiled then, as if tired. Outside it was a lovely late-summer day. The other students were emerging, shouting and laughing, into daylight.

On the way home, Rheya and I rode in silence. She refused to talk about the incident or about her suspension, shrugged off even my scolding. Only when we were halfway home did she speak. 'I saw Melissa's parents today.'

I glanced over at her. 'When?'

'Back in the principal's office. They came by after the memorial.'

I kept my eyes on the road.

'They want to enshrine her,' she said. 'The funeral's on Monday. Right before they turn over the body.'

'Would you like to go?'

She shrugged and looked outside. 'Everyone at school keeps talking,' she said. 'About how great she was. What good friends they were. Half of them didn't even know her. Half of them didn't even like her.'

'They're just upset.'

'They didn't even know her,' she repeated. She glared out the window. 'They're all just pretending. All the other girls keep crying, keep on making a big show of it. I hate it. I hate them.' We drove on then for a few minutes in silence, after which she asked, 'Do you think dying hurts?'

I didn't know how to respond.

'What if she remembers?' she asked. 'I mean Melissa. How it all happened?'

'She won't remember,' I said. For once I didn't have to lie. My sister only remembers the fatal night up to a certain point: rehearsing for the play, our father picking her up. It is only when asked about what came next, or how she thinks she got home, that the frightening realisations start to come. I have learned to shield her from these moments, as one might shield a daughter, or an aging parent. 'I can lend you my receiver,' I said. 'Show you how to tune it. Then you can go see Melissa whenever you want.' My daughter didn't respond. Instead she stared outside as we drove. The trees and streets passed over her reflection, like clouds.

Inside the render, I always come upon my sister in the middle of things: in the park perhaps, or on a beach we visited as children. Sometimes I find her upstairs, in her old bedroom, leafing through the pages of a book. What was she reading, I wonder? Would it even matter now? I have never been brave enough to ask.

After bringing my daughter home, I went to visit Mira. I entered the render, arrived in our childhood home to find it deserted. It was afternoon sometime; the sun was playing on the leaves outside. I paused in the hallway, saw my face reflected in the mirror: the tired gaze, the crow's feet. I closed my eyes and tried to remember the smell of the hardwood floors, the feel of the old wallpaper beneath my fingertips. When I opened my eyes, the world was a size larger. My face was a child's once again. At the window a hummingbird flew up. I watched it hover, watched it cock its head to look at me. Behind me then, a sound of footsteps.

'I'm home!' said Mira. She pulled the screen door open, kicked off her shoes, went to take her book bag upstairs. She stopped when she saw me, held a moment, grinned. 'Hey,' she said. 'What's up? Where are Mom and Dad?'

I smiled. They are so good, these moments, when everything for a brief spell is normal again. The feeling never lasts. Where were our parents? Our father was of course in the nursing home; our mother, interred in a memorial garden outside of Seattle. I affected a childish tone then, invented some story about errands and our father being back in the garage. My sister has never been one to question such things. She shrugged and went to head upstairs, until I called out after her. 'Wait.'

She stopped.

'Maybe we could hang out,' I said. 'Maybe read books together or something?'

My sister said nothing. Hidden thoughts turned behind her arresting blue eyes. 'Cleo, I've got homework,' she said. 'Not right now. Maybe later this evening, alright?' Then she was gone up the stairs. I stood there a moment in the silence, reached up and pulled out my earbuds. I woke in my own bed with a sharp intake of breath, sat up and placed my feet upon the floor. At the window, a sudden flicker of motion: another hummingbird. I watched it dart back and forth around the feeder. It took no notice of me.

Several days ago, I came in from my morning run. I called upstairs. 'Rheya, are you up?' It was three days into her suspension. When she didn't respond I poured myself a shake, went upstairs, showered and retreated into my bedroom. I brought out my receiver, seeking out the soft comfort of the render. When I entered however, I was surprised to hear what sounded like laughter. I put on the girlish face of my youth, called out in a child's voice, 'Mira?' We were back in the park again. I followed the sound of the merriment to its source, to a grove of tall pines just off the path. At the base of a tree, two girls were sitting on the bench. There were differences between them of course — their ages, their hairstyles, the colouring of their eyes — but there was no mistaking them. Even the way they craned their necks to look came in eerie unison. My first terrified thought was *Does she know?* followed immediately by *Would it even matter?* I recovered then, stood and straightened. 'Rheya, what is this?' I asked. 'What are you doing here?'

My daughter frowned. It must have surprised her to see me as my younger self, but eventually the realisation dawned. 'Mom?' As soon as the words were spoken she disappeared. She had obviously severed her connection. Mira quickly noticed the absence, became aware that something was amiss. 'Rheya?' she said. 'Cleo, what's going on? I don't understand.'

'Go back to sleep,' I said. 'Everything's fine.' I exited the render myself, got out of bed and went straight into Rheya's room. I entered to find her quickly closing a drawer. She spun.

'What were you doing?' I asked. 'What was that? I never gave you permission to go in there.'

My daughter frowned. 'We were just talking,' she said. 'I wasn't hurting anything. I'd just never talked to a dead person before.'

'What about your friend Melissa?' Her face crumpled. When you have lived with grief so long it can be easy to forget the rawness of it. I changed the subject then, asked her, 'Where did you get a receiver?'

'I borrowed it from Ariel,' she said. 'Her parents never use theirs. I looked online for how to tune it. I got the frequency off of yours.'

'Do they know that you took it?'

Rheya shook her head.

'You're grounded for another week,' I said. 'I'll be sure to have a talk with Ariel's parents.' I confiscated the receiver, went back into my room and put it up with my own. I would have to buy a lock, I decided, or find some other way to secure my things.

I sat down on my bed, rubbed at my temples with my fingers. Wondered, what relics do we keep of those we love: a photograph, an archived memory, a lock of hair? When are they no longer enough? I listened as my daughter wept into her pillow down the hall. It is never enough, I remember thinking. There is no such thing as enough.

Several days later I went back to visit Mira. She had forgotten entirely about the incident with Rheya. The dead are not like us, understand: they do not learn new things, cannot form new memories. They have become read-only in a sense, but because my sister still remembers me from life, she will remember me — at least as I used to be — forever. My daughter will never be more than a stranger.

In the render, we were up at our family's lakeshore cabin. It was autumn, in the evening sometime. Along the shore, the waters were very gentle. The sun moved queerly through the trees, following us as we walked. Mira said:

'I never get tired of all this.'

I smiled. 'It's nice,' I said. We kept on walking, and I savoured the smell of leaves, the crisp mossy bite to the air. Mira spoke up again.

'I wish that Dad would come out and see it.'

'I know.' I have learned to speak carefully at such moments. It can be fearfully easy to upset the dead; they are much like the elderly, or like very small children. 'He's just busy.'

'He's always busy,' she said. She glanced back toward the cabin. 'Always holed up inside his study. I keep telling him we should spent more time together, that we won't always have these moments, but he only ever tells me "later." Always "later".'

I frowned. On a surface level, I knew she was simply trapped in the memory of being alive, but to hear her speak so? There are times when I fear that, even subconsciously, she is aware of what has happened to her. 'I just miss him,' she said. 'That's all.'

'I know,' I said. 'I miss him too.'

The rest of that evening was uneventful: dinner in silence with Rheya, loading up the dishwasher, grading papers. All the while I was haunted by what Mira had said. I wondered: could it be too late to bring her and my father back together? I remembered what the doctor had said, about dementia being a barrier to enshrinement, but what if the memories jogged something loose? Could it be a way to slow the path of the disease? Perhaps I could give Mira what she had been missing. I had to act, I decided. I had to try, for all our sakes.

The following day I prepared for my weekly visit to the nursing home. I gathered up my receiver, along with a small pair of speakers. I took my purse and keys off the dresser, made to head downstairs. I paused as I passed my daughter's room; her door was partway open, and I spied her sitting on her bed. She had her computer open in front of her, and onscreen was a collage of photos. Melissa smiling, Melissa in a Santa Claus hat, Melissa and Rheya together on a class trip. At some point Rheya became aware of my presence, looked up. I went to speak only to find the words caught inside my throat. Instead I looked away and headed on downstairs. There are certain burdens that the act of speaking can only make heavier.

At the nursing home, I moved quietly. It was a sleepy afternoon among the common areas and mint-green hallways, and I found my father in his usual state, curled foetal in his bed by the window. I kissed his cheek and sat down by his side, began reaching into my purse for the receiver and speakers. I set them up on my father's nightstand, smiled as his eyes followed me. 'Where's Mira?' he asked. 'When is Mira coming home?'

'Soon,' I said. 'Don't you worry.' I went and closed the door, sat back down, turned up the volume on the speakers. Before long the room had faded away, replaced instead by the long front walk of our old home. It was early afternoon, and the day was washed in that familiar grey light. My sister was reading on the porch swing. I looked to my father, whose eyes and mouth worked soundlessly. 'Dad?' I said. 'Go say hi.' A flicker of motion caught my eye then, and I was distracted very briefly. When I looked back again, my father was walking up the porch, but his hair was thicker, darker, his bearing more that of the man I'd grown up with. He crested the steps then as a man of forty, and Mira hopped up out of the hammock to embrace him. I smiled. In that one moment we were normal again. I approached them both, and when they turned to face me that flicker of motion came again. Suddenly the man embracing my sister was replaced by a boy, barely a teenager. Another flicker and he was a man in his thirties. 'Dad?' I said. The curse of Alzheimer's is to relive one's life out of sequence. By now I was growing frightened. I asked him, 'Are you alright?'

'Mira?' he asked. He was looking straight at me instead of her. 'Mira, where are we? What's going on? I want to go see my Mira.'

'Cleo?' My sister looked at both of us. 'What's going on? What's happening?'

'Mira,' I said. 'Go back inside. Everything's fine.' There came the flicker again and suddenly my father was old once more; he looked at my sister and clutched at her arm. There were tears streaking down his cheeks, and soon he embraced her, and began to weep. 'Mira,' he said.

'Dad?' She struggled against his embrace. 'Cleo, help. Get him off me. You're scaring me.'

'Stop it,' I said. I reached in and tried to pull him off, but his grip was stronger than mine. He fought me, saying 'no,' and starting to sob. I said to him, 'Dad, you need to wake up,' but by then it was too late. The sky and the trees were changing. The light took on a disturbing hue. Soon Mira was crying as well, saying 'no,' saying 'please.'

'Just relax,' I said. 'It's fine, everything's fine.'

'Get away!' she screamed. The render split into bizarre and frightening new architectures. A firm hand abruptly gripped my shoulder, and then we were back in the nursing home. An orderly was pulling me to my feet; a team of nurses and caretakers had yanked out the speakers, were struggling to get my father under sedation. He was sobbing, even as he fought them. 'Mira,' he said, 'Mira, please.'

Afterward, I walked out in a daze. My footsteps echoed in the halls, and at some point I realised I was being followed. 'Ms Shelley,' a female voice called out. 'Ms Shelley, I'd like to speak with you a moment.'

I ignored the woman's commands and kept walking.

'Ms Shelley,' she said. I got to the main lobby doors before the locks clicked shut in front of me. I stopped and shook my head, turned to face my accuser. It was the head nurse. She was elegantly middle-aged, dressed in blue scrubs and a cardigan. She had blue eyes and lovely cheekbones, and when she spoke her voice was very calm. She did not smile.

'I should have you walked off the premises and not allowed back,' she said. 'People are resting. This is supposed to be a quiet place.'

'Do what you like,' I said. My eyes suddenly felt hot; I looked out the window to conceal my guilt. When some moments had passed, the nurse merely sighed and unlocked the doors.

'Just go,' she said.

'Thank you.' I turned on my heels and left. Most things in life are never resolved, I have found. They are simply given up.

I came home to find Rheya reading downstairs in the living room: I had requested the doors be rekeyed, so as to prevent her from leaving the house. I left my purse on the table, went to the sink and poured myself a glass of water. I felt her in the doorway behind me, watching. 'Mom,' she said. 'Mom.'

'I need a moment,' I said. 'Please.' She said nothing in response, and so I believed the conversation was finished. I went into the living room, stood and stared out the window. Then from the kitchen I heard a sound of things being rifled: a brief crash, a muffled shriek. 'Rheya?' I headed back then to find my purse spilled upon the floor, with what remained of my receiver lying shattered against the far wall. My daughter was stomping on it, screaming, crushing the remnants into ever-smaller pieces. I told her to stop, grabbed her and went to restrain her. After a brief struggle though she stopped resisting, gripped me instead with all of her strength. She buried her face into my chest, collapsed hard into my arms. After a moment I allowed myself to return her embrace, to squeeze her and stroke her hair and tell her, 'No, sweetie, no. I'm here. It's okay.' Her shoulders shook. When the sob escaped it was quiet, like the sound of a glass breaking.

Many of the ghost stories we see here at The Fiction Desk involve academics: they are almost always dry, earnest, curious but reserved, male. Even in stories with a modern setting, as often as not they're just Edwardians with iPhones. In the real world of the twenty-first century, however, you're more likely to bump into a postgraduate a little more like Bethany.

The Crypt Beneath the Library

Barney Walsh

The university's moderately impressive collection of rare medieval codices and curiosities is held, alongside much else, in a separate sub-library in the city centre, far from the main campus. This building, squeezed incongruously between the shiny glass and steel structures of modern retail and finance, is a church-like neo-Gothic thing of reddish-black stone, made complex with crenellations and other fiddly fancy bits, finials and scalloping and curlicues (or is that just handwriting?), and lots of little tiny gargoyles and grotesques way up high so they're hard to make out from the street, where Bethany's standing now, one hand shielding her eyes from the winter's low sun.

The library has tall, pointy stained-glass windows, criss-crossed with lead, and huge thick black wooden doors that must take a long, creaking minute to slam in your infidel face. It's a bit of a mishmash maybe, though architecture is not Bethany's field and her specialism is way earlier: she's a medieval girl, while this was built only in the nineteenth century, if she's remembering rightly. Later, the building was a philanthropic industrialist's acquisition and donation to the people of the city, intended a bit vaguely to support the education of the region's cotton workers, which noble aim got maybe kind of neglected. It was practically derelict, and with several strange and unpleasant stories circulating about it — certainly one murder was recorded to have taken place in its grounds — when the university took it over some time after the war. Now it's where they keep their poshest, oldest books, along with a desultory museum of northern industry, some local-interest stuff, a little art gallery, other bits and bobs of donations. There's a big collection of old theological texts, plus some really ancient scraps of Hebrew bible and the disintegrating scrolls of a gnostic gospel or two. There's a roomful somewhere of Egyptian scarabs and sarcophagi, cursed whatnots and crumbly chunks of statues; in some crypt or other under the library there's supposed to be the tomb of this ancient tribal warrior woman or something, dug up and dragged here from God knows where. Things like that, nothing to go mad over.

You get in, disappointingly, not through the big oak doors with their massive, fuck-ugly knockers — they're fenced off now — but through a recently added annexe, all brushed metal and tinted glass, which Bethany's got to guess the spirits of the place kind of hate. But after a bit of bureaucracy she gets through to the gloom of the library proper, into the long reading room, which you'd swear was meant for a church if you didn't know better, flanked by arched aisles with galleries above them, all under a high vaulted ceiling with details picked out in fading gold leaf. Long lancet windows at either end. What's not old stone is dark, gleaming oak floorboards and wall panels, long tables, and chairs cushioned in threadbare green stuff. There are maybe half a dozen readers in place already, all men as it happens, sitting as far from one another as possible; two or three eye Bethany as she comes in, heads bobbing up from behind green glass lampshades. Her heels tap too noisily on the uncarpeted floorboards, casting little echoes all through the place; next time she'll wear something with a softer sole.

To get at the texts she wants, Bethany had to provide a letter from her PhD supervisor, along with quite a long account of why she can't work from digital scans and transcripts like everyone else. They bring the fragile old texts she wants one by one from their atmospherically controlled vault or cupboard; the librarian would probably ask her not even to breathe while she's reading if he could. She has to wear thin cotton gloves to turn the pages, though she's really tempted to remove one, just to be the first person in centuries or more to touch the old pigments, the inky ridges of the lettering. She's a good girl though, sticks to the agreement she's signed. She ties back her hair. The book is a bestiary, a medieval catalogue of creatures real and mythical – the distinction evidently not very clear back then, as the two fill these pages on an equal footing. On the recto you'll find nothing more exotic than a zebra, but then there's this worm – a coiled, serpent-like kind of dragon, it looks like, with tiny vestigial wings – waiting to surprise you on the verso. A hippo glares fearfully at a griffon; a tiger (is it a tiger; its stripes are so weird and wiggly?) cavorts with a centaur. Done before anyone had figured out the laws of perspective, they're sort of quaint in their flatness and simplicity, but then kind of horrible in their freakishness, even to Bethany's trained eye. The worst is maybe the basilisk: this black, reptilian kind of four-legged rooster, a grotesque thing with a scaly hooked tail, its wild bulgy eyes beaming pale light over a bunch of Chaucerian pilgrims, sending them one by one reeling and turning to stone, falling to shatter on the ground. Unusual dynamism for a medieval illumination; she makes a note. Another note: *Yuck!*

Even the real ones were obviously inked by someone who's been given no reliable description of an animal he's never seen and can't really visualise. A lion has a big bulbous head and a crimson mane that flows all down its back, pouring in a twin-pointed beard off its thrust-forward chin. Its face looks almost human. A rhino is weirdly inflected with unicorn blood, or vice versa: too bulky and armour-plated for one, too equine in the face and dainty in the long, clip-clopping legs for the other. *All* the eyes look human, and gaze at you straight on, like in Egyptian hieroglyphics. There's some deranged zoology going on here, all right.

A couple of hours is about all she can bear. Bethany's just about to pack it in for the day when something a tiny bit odd happens. She's closed up the bestiary; a librarian's coming to reseal it in its hermetic home. She finishes a note and with her free hand massages the muscles at the base of her neck (all this book-time is bad for your joints, your posture). Takes one last idle glance about the room, fatigue-numbed now to its beauty – and then she sees it, in the light just over a window ledge: a little storm of dust, swirling in a breeze, maybe from a crack in the frame. The afternoon's last light picks out every mote. A tiny cloud tumbling over itself. And then, just for a moment, there's a face in it. A long nose and the pits of two eyes; the twist of a mouth. It's only there for a millisecond. Probably she imagined it. The breeze dies and the dust settles, or disperses.

Huh.

Whose ashes were those? Probably she imagined it all. Must have done. A face, looking right at her. Though of course you can see fake patterns in randomness. It's weird, though. It didn't seem a way that dust or ash is meant to move in, that's all.

It's a relief to be on her feet again, to straighten her back, to get out into the air, cold as the world is right now. She gets the bus home, noisy and hot with schoolkids, commuters. Her boyfriend's not back from work yet. She dumps her stuff, kicks off her heels. Had enough of the twelfth century for one day, let's try a bit of the twenty-first. She checks her emails, kills an hour on Facebook. Her boyfriend texts: he's held up at work again, sorry. He'd better not be cheating on her — but she knows he's not. It's just work. She starts a stir-fry, opens a bottle of wine, puts music on loud. Veggies sizzle and pop in olive oil. It's only when she closes her eyes, at odd brief moments, that she sees the strange monsters and mutants have followed her home. She has two glasses of wine, a bit too much of a head start on her boyfriend, really. It's an evening for a box set binge. She's a bit worried about the night, the creatures in the book being terrific nightmare fuel — not to mention the ghastly face, which she remembers with perfect clarity even though she saw or imagined it for so brief a spell. But in the end, after a gentle fuck with her boyfriend (he's started being that much more tender, now that she's finally told him what happened to her), all she does is sleep eight solid hours of totally dreamless sleep. In the morning she's almost disappointed not to have been visited by horrors.

She can't resist: the inks are just too *juicy*. She glances about to see no one's watching, and seeing all the other readers' heads are tipped safely into their books, she peels off one glove and touches the many-centuries-old vellum with her bare hand. Very gently she strokes the thick black lettering of a page, the gilt and verdigris and vermilion of a lovely historiated initial showing some saint being martyred. He's upside down and nailed to the large T that starts the page's text, his guts spilling from his abdomen and parting into two streams to pour down either side of his face and pool below him, the blood sprouting into flowers at the edges. She puts her glove back on. She'd have to look up which martyr he is; it's not like she has them at her fingertips. She could Google it — the library has free Wi-Fi and her tablet's right there in her bag — but any post-Gutenberg technology would feel kind of obscene in this place, not to say blasphemous. She makes her notes in a thick spiral-bound pad, will type them up and add extra thoughts later at home. Ought to be using a quill.

Today's tome is an illuminated Gospel of Luke combined with an Acts of the Apostles, both being supposedly by the one author; but in which she's finding, weirdly, that the images don't match the words. The parable of the Good Samaritan is illustrated, totally inappropriately, by a gang of men crowded aggressively around a woman who seems to be talking (prophesying?), but they're really not liking what she has to say; while the loaves-and-fishes stuff has a child — girl or boy it's hard to tell — sitting on this dead or sleeping man's chest and eating what might be his heart, might be a cheeseburger. She also finds a funny illumination of Doubting Thomas, though she happens to know that disciple's scepticism is in John, not Luke: as he presses his fingers to Christ's wounds they come out the other side, blood falling in stylised droplets with (she thinks) little laughing faces in them. Again there are the tiny flowers growing from the puddle.

There's a John the Baptist with, as you'd expect, his head on a plate; but the long locks of his hair turn Medusa-like into snakes that begin to crawl across the floor. What can *that* mean? There's a beardless Christ — looks like a woman, actually — smiling down from the cross, a huge extra nail piercing his or her rounded (pregnant?) belly. There is some insanely blasphemous shit going down in this book. Bethany *loves* it. How come it's not famous, this book: why hasn't it been discussed in any of the books, essays, articles that's she's looked at in her researches? Can seriously no other scholars have had a look? Certainly it'll go into her thesis, might change the whole course of the thing; because what kind of nut was doing this, in the eleven or twelve hundreds, and how'd they get away with it? Plus for sure she can get a paper or two published out of it. She hopes her supervisor won't try to hijack too much of the credit.

She gently turns the pages, fascinated, and then almost cries out. Claps her fingers over her lips, looks around guiltily to be sure she'd not actually made a noise and embarrassed herself in front of all these studious people. She almost laughs at herself instead. It startled her, that's all, a ... a monster, a *thing*, kind of leaping out at her. They'd not done pop-up books in medieval times; what a missed opportunity. Now she does give one nervous laugh. The librarian at his desk across the room frowns at her; she bends her eyes back to the horrible thing.

Again, it's dropped into the text seemingly at random: it's not alongside the bit about the Devil from the Temptations in the Wilderness or anything that would kind of seem appropriate, and doesn't anyway much resemble what she thinks the devil is meant to look like. It's white, not red or black. Naked and almost hairless — just a few yellowish wisps about its skull, arms and shoulders — terribly emaciated but strong, you somehow feel. It's quite small, as if it were an intruder on the page, stalking in from the margins; but the page's lettering makes space for it, as if recoiling from the sight. A creeping thing, limbed like a human but almost on all fours, and with a tail. It's oddly beautiful, though. After a bit you see the ... well, *attraction* is the wrong word. She draws a gloved finger down its white lead limbs. Then, after checking there's still no one snooping on her, she slips off a glove (last time, she promises), to touch the old, old pigments with her bare skin, as maybe no one's done in centuries. A monster: demon, elemental, ghoul? She'd have to research types of ... types of unholy *thing*, find out which one's this. Find out why it's here. The illumination feels oddly cold. A little shiver runs up her spine. Why is it the really grotesque ones that attract her? Better not tell her boyfriend that: he's not grotesque. He's lovely, capable of being really sweet when she can get hold of all his attention.

But this time she knows instantly she's been caught. She can feel this disapproving glare, actually this look of pure hatred, coming from she doesn't know where. She snatches back her hand, slides it under the table to yank the glove back into place, finger by finger. She looks around guiltily. A naughty schoolgirl, caught – but caught by whom? All the other readers are still absorbed in their words; no stern librarians hover to kick her out for disrespecting the priceless volumes. Still there's the pressure of this gaze on her. She lifts her eyes, looks up; and there, in one of the galleries that line the reading room, half veiled in shadow, a man looks down at her. Her eyes meet his just for a moment before his gaze bats hers away. She looks back to the page; then slowly, helplessly looks up again. The man is bald, very tall and thin. As far as she can see he's dressed entirely in black, with what look like the folds of a hood lowered about his shoulders. His cheeks are gaunt; he looks very pale, but not ill. He leans forwards over the gallery's balustrade and surveys the library, his domain, spread out below him. His eyes sweep up and back down the reading-room area before settling once more on Bethany. Again their eyes meet. This time she holds on to his stern gaze, until slowly, after a long moment or two, he withdraws unblinking into the darkness of the gallery.

She's getting better at reading Middle English, even in the more offbeat dialects, navigating its thorns and thickets, but still it's headache inducing. After hours of peering at the dense, crabbed, bleeding inks of centuries ago, she needs a break. There's a little deserted café; after a while this hostile little witch appears, acts all affronted at Bethany's request for a cup of tea. Bethany can't stay long under that glare either, but when she rises to head back to the reading room she finds herself taking a wrong turning, deliberately getting lost. There's a narrow spiral staircase: cold stone walls with wooden treads that sag perceptibly underfoot. Does this lead to the gallery? Does she want to risk meeting that creepy guy? If he's even real. But it's not the gallery: it's more books, just what she needs. Room after room of them. The small, high windows, threaded with lead and tucked between bookcases, let in pale sunbeams that dance with dust in the gloom. One roomful of books bending into another, the doors never quite placed in the wall as you'd think they'd be — was the architect a bit mad, or was this bit of the building just cobbled together totally aimlessly? Always there's an unexpected step or three down, or up. She can't quite figure out where in the library she is; the windows are too high and misty with age for you to look through to see the street and get your bearings. She strokes the dusty spines as she passes. She knows the building's nowhere near old enough but these rooms feel like no one's set foot in them for hundreds of years, like they're just as they were in the twelfth, eleventh, tenth century. A library within a library. The codices she's working on could have been created here. Bored monks painstakingly inking the letters, the images. What were they thinking?

She has to keep reminding herself that the building's nowhere near that old. It's the words that carry the years, not the stones.

She pulls a volume from a wall at random: its dense two-columned pages are in German, not one of her tongues; the date's eighteenth century. She tries another: this one's in English, a commentary on or rejection of something-or-other of Augustine's. Another: a detailed refutation of certain unsound views on the nature of the Trinity. This must be the famous theology collection. No wonder there's no one here. Not quite Bethany's field: too recent, too silly. She's an atheist medievalist. Not that she's against a good battle between orthodoxy and heresy, but they're more fun when someone could get burned at the stake for his stupid beliefs. All these tomes are too safe and theoretical; none of the writers thought they might die for what they were saying. You can't spend months and years amid such old books without getting a little bit morbid. She liked these rooms better when she didn't know what was in the books; they've lost some of their mystery now. So: back to work.

She turns, retraces her steps, and comes to a dead end. Oh. Bit of a maze, this place. She goes back, takes a left instead of a right, comes to another dead end, a blank wall of books. Okay. Resists the temptation to note one of the titles, so she can check next time that she's not returning to the same spot. The place isn't *that* big. Then she hears footsteps, coming towards her. A slow, even tread. Creak, creak. Creak. Someone coming to rescue her. If she needed it, which she doesn't. Her own comfy soft boots make almost no noise on the boards.

Okay. She moves through the twists and turns of the bookcase-filled rooms, heading towards the slow-creaking footsteps, takes another wrong turn, and another (seriously, is this place for real?), until she rounds a final corner, preparing a smile, in case she's not supposed to be in here. *Sorry, I got a bit lost* ... and there's no one there. The footsteps stop on the instant. She has the place all to herself.

Weird.

Could it have been an echo, or a creak coming from the floor above? But it stopped so exactly as she came round the final corner. And now there's just this total creepy stillness. Whoever was there walking has gone now. Vanished. Or is here and unseen, watching. And as soon as Bethany thinks that, the sense of being watched is irresistible. It's funny, why do our minds do these things to us? She stands there a moment longer to enjoy it: the sense of invisible eyes, malignant, watching her. A totally made-up feeling, she does know that. But then after a bit it's too much, wherever it's coming from, and she hurries back to the main reading room — finds her way no problem now — back to the people.

Signing in and out every day, she's been saying hi to the old security guard on the door, passing a few pointless remarks, lifting him from his paperback crime novel, letting him amiably flirt at her. Now as she's leaving, she has to ask.

'Ghosts?' says the guard. 'Oh yeah, love, there's ghosts aplenty in this place. Which do you want to know about: the grey woman, the murdered scholar, the blasphemous monk, the little lost child, the headless someone-or-other?'

A monk? The bald man's black hood maybe could've been part of a monk's get-up, she guesses. Which orders wore black?

'What have you seen?' she asks.

'Bugger all,' says the guard. 'I'm one of them Enlightenment thinkers, me. No silly superstitions in this head.'

'Okay, good. But tell me anyway, who's the ... the grey woman?' She doesn't know what stopped her asking about the monk.

The grey lady? Well, she's just a girl really. And grey. Silver might have been more poetic, but grey seems to have stuck. She's just this young girl. Victorian, you know. Long dress. Wanders the place at night. And in the day too, maybe, but you only ever see her at night, as if she only shows up by moon or starlight. She's just this dim blurry shape really, could be anything. Allegedly the daughter of the nutty architect who had the place built. Anyway she disappeared at about the right time, that much is historical record. Maybe she ran off with a mule spinner, a love crossing class boundaries. But diabolical human sacrifice, goes the story. Supposedly the guy — a diabolist, is that the word? — laced the cement of the place with the blood of his virgin daughter. As you do. *Why* exactly is anyone's guess. Nefarious occult practices, one presumes. So every stone of the library is held in place by her blood, her flesh, her soul — so that both will last forever, maybe. That kind of thing. Though it sounds sort of impractical, come to think of it. I mean, how much blood can there be in one little girl? They would've had to slaughter dozens, really. But there you go. And so all she does is wander about the place at night, unable to leave because she is built into the place now for all eternity, totally lost and bewildered because she never actually saw the library when she was alive, doesn't know where she is, doesn't know *what* she is.

That's about it. Utter bollocks, of course. Cheery little tale, though, isn't it? Bethany says yeah, thanks, got to be going now. She hurries out to the wintry street, shivers. Snow soon, maybe. She glances over her shoulder, just once, looking for spectral faces watching her from the library's windows. There's nothing. Probably anyway the old guy was making it all up on the spot.

The world outside the library churns on as always. Bethany works through her notes, highlights key points. She sees her supervisor. Goes to the cinema with her boyfriend: an awful, blood-spattered horror movie loaded with tedious jump-scares and all the other old tricks she's seen so often before. She meets friends for drinks, Skypes her parents. She runs in the cold misty mornings, the local park's lawns almost tinkling with frost. Her boyfriend gets dead upset when he misses out on a promotion he felt entitled to, and which secretly Bethany reckoned he wasn't ready for; she consoles him as best she can. He goes out alone to get drunk with his mates. She drinks wine and reads and looks at the moonlight illuminating the year's first thin dusting of snow.

'How is it?' her boyfriend asks over breakfast one morning, finally thinking to ask after her work, not that he considers it work: it's just reading all day, plus he finds it kind of silly that she'd still want to be a student, linger at university so long, not get out into the real world.

'Oh, you know,' she says. 'Boring.'

'Careful,' he says. 'It's what you're after doing with the rest of your life.'

'Boring to you, I mean. Me, I love it. The creak of the leather on a really old book, the delicate crackle of pages that feel like they'll crumble if you just look at the letters too hard. The little pained noises of an old book's spine opening for the first time in decades. The specks of dust glittering in a beam of light. The smells, God, don't even get me started on the smells. The old paper and brittle glue and weird mustiness, no two books quite alike —'

'Okay, okay,' says her boyfriend. 'Sorry I asked.' And he really is, you can tell. 'I get the picture,' he says. 'You know, you're a bit weird sometimes.' He laughs. His eyes have hardly risen from his smartphone.

'Let's talk about something else,' she says. That shuts him up.

There's a shadow that shouldn't be there. Across the room from Bethany, farther down the long wall on a patch of unpanelled stone, a shadow slowly rises where there's no light to cast it. The room's reading lamps are too weak, too low to throw so stark a shadow. The shape seems to flicker slightly, as if cast by rushlight or candle flame. It's the figure of a man, rising up the stonework as if from a grave. As it reaches its full height she sees how misshapen it is.

It slides along the wall, rippling over bookcases, over the leather spines. Then when it's directly opposite Bethany it begins to detach itself from the wall: a hand, arm, shoulder … a head. A shadow cast on air. The skull on its long neck twists this way and that. It moves awkwardly, slowly. It takes a juddering step away from the wall, towards Bethany, its arm reaching impossibly for her.

She doesn't panic. The thing's moving slowly; she has plenty of time. She closes today's codex — just a boring old catalogue; she's been trying to trace the provenance of the weird stuff she looked at, but can't find any references to it anywhere. She calmly rises, gathers up her notes and stuffs them into her bag, turns and walks to the exit. The librarian will come to collect the book. Just as if everything were totally normal, she signs herself out, says goodnight to the old security guard. At the door she turns back and looks: the walls, the bookshelves, are bare now of any misplaced shadows; nothing dark floats on the air.

The relief of it. The city's crowds: business types flowing hither and thither; homeless people going nowhere. All the traffic belching and bellowing at itself. A queue at a cash machine, people smoking outside bars. The glass wall of a shop full of designer dresses she can't afford. Just stupid *life*.

She hits the nearest wine bar, gets halfway down a big glass of Merlot before calling her boyfriend to come meet her when he's done at work. Something in her voice must've got through to him for once: he turns up surprisingly quick, can't normally get away so readily.

'What's up?' he says. 'On the phone you sounded kind of —'

She interrupts: 'Let's just get drunk, okay?'

'Well all right then.'

They're out all evening, both getting pretty wrecked; he must've called some mates at some point because suddenly they're in a crowd, the bar's packed and noisy and there's no room for thought. She tries to drown the memory of what she thought she saw, what she's pretty sure now she didn't see. Must have imagined it: books do funny things to your head, sometimes. God knows what time it is when they stagger into a cab, tumble home, topple into bed. Somehow they manage to have sex, pissed as they are; and it's good, it helps, her boyfriend's ordinary, slightly clumsy physicality, his sweaty fleshiness. It drowns her mind's buzzing just for a few minutes, enough maybe that she'll sleep.

She wakes from a dream to find herself alone in the library at night. She opens her eyes. Her cheek is pressed flat to the vellum. Lifts her head. She must've dozed off. God. Her pen still pinched between her fingers. What time is it? Hope she didn't drool in the book: they really frown on stuff like that. It's dark. Not just that the daylight has failed from the long windows at either end of the hall: all the electric lights are out, too. There's only the moon slicing palely in. It's really quiet: usually there's some slight shuffling of papers, the scritch-scratch of someone's fountain pen. But this is the deepest silence she's ever known. She looks around. Everyone else is gone. She's fallen asleep and got locked in. That idiot guard didn't even check, after all the flirty attention he's shown before.

Again she stays consciously calm. She leaves her stuff, goes to the door to the new annexe, the way in and way out. It's locked. Okay. There's a fire exit in the corner — push the bar, it says, but the bar is locked in place. Okay, great. That's really got to be against some regulations. There are the original huge oak doors, of course, but they're not even worth trying: probably she couldn't even lift the great iron handle, never mind swing the vast wooden wall of a door. She goes to her bag, wakes up her phone – and the thing's dead. The battery's died. Course she's not got a charger, course she's not brought her tablet today, when really she does need some post-Gutenberg tech.

Shit.

She stands at the table, glances down at the book that put her to sleep – and it's the demon or elemental again. Of course it is. But is it the same one? It's bigger, surely: it fills the page, all the words have fled. She had her cheek rested on it, like on a lover's chest. And then she sees that the image is moving. It raises it body, straightens its arched back. Its limbs twist towards her; its mouth opens, showing its teeth.

Bethany yelps, slams the book shut.

Too loud. It will have woken something.

Don't be silly. There's nothing.

But anyway she can't stand here in the dark all night. And she's not about to just wait for the security guard to unlock the doors in the morning and let her out. Maybe she can find another exit; even a window she can get open, a window she can break – but they're all tiny panes, in immoveable lead frames.

She doesn't know where to go. Not back up to the theology library, there was no way out there. She's trying to think ... and then the books begin to whisper. She hears it coming from all around her, passing through the walls from wherever there are books living. Every word that's locked within them softly spoken all at once. It's so quiet, and deafening. She puts her hands to her ears but it makes no difference. She tries another door; it won't open. And then one whisper begins to get louder than the others: a voice, of something walking through the library, getting closer. Looking for her.

The only thing to do is go and meet it.

At the far end of the reading room, twin flights of staircase turn towards the room's long, arched galleries. The dark oaken treads creak lightly underfoot, cold as stone on her toes; she's barefoot, she suddenly realises. She doesn't go back for her shoes. She takes the left flight, towards the whispering. There's only a pale, diffuse light coming through the tall windows – shouldn't there be a city out there, with all its people, its late-night noise? But there's only the whispering, getting louder, more insistent as she gets closer, and the creaking underfoot. The staircase turns back on itself through one half-landing then another, and then she's at the top. At the far end of the gallery, the black-robed figure waits for her. Whispering softly, as if to himself – but it's for her. It's all for her. He's facing away from her, his hood raised now to cover his skull. She could turn and run – try to find a door or a window she can get open, or an office with a phone she can use to call for help – or she could do just what she's doing, and walk softly towards the figure. It doesn't move. It knows she's there. It's waiting.

She steps slowly closer, and as she reaches it, it turns to her. Its robes flutter and flow, spread wide. The thing embraces her, its face a brief flurry of leering dust in an empty hood. The robes in their blackness envelop her. All air is gone, all light is gone. There's only the dust and the darkness. And she accepts these gifts.

She comes awake from this dream to find herself at home in bed, twisted in sweaty sheets, her naked boyfriend snoring beside her. It's getting light; a hangover thumps in her skull. She sits up in bed, shivering and hugging her knees to herself, watching the morning's light slowly illuminating the window, till her boyfriend wakes and sees her there.

'What's up?' he says.

'Nothing,' she says. 'A stupid, freaky dream, that's all.'

'About me?'

'You wish.'

She lies in bed for a long time after he's left for work. Eventually she pulls herself to her feet. She does some work from home, a different kind of research — academic journals, stuff like that, dry but not dusty, reads them on her laptop in bed. She expands her notes for her literature review. She gets out her phone, goes through the few people she knows in this city till she finds one who can meet her for lunch: she moved away from most of her friends when she came up north to do her PhD. Later she has a tutorial with her thesis supervisor. He asks after her researches among the codices, but she's just vague in reply, evasive; as if she's disappointed, and not found much of interest.

She goes back to the old library one last time. She asks again for the first book she looked at, the bestiary. She gently turns the brittle pages. All the old familiar beasts. None of them seem to have moved. She finds again the monster, the demon, elemental, whatever it is. Hello. This time, breaking the rules — you're meant to get written permission — she takes out her phone and grabs a picture of it. The phone's glass doesn't crack or anything. She thinks she can feel that shadow sliding towards her again, but she doesn't look up to check; doesn't look either to see if the bald man, the corrupt monk or whatever he is, is there on the balcony.

Then she scrolls almost at random through her phone's contacts list before settling, maybe inevitably, on the scumbag professor, one of her tutors from the university far across the country where somehow she got through her BA. He's still listed in there as 'Professor', despite having become so much more than that — and then abruptly so much less. And he's not a professor anymore; still hadn't got another job, last she heard. Of course they'd sacked him. He could've gone to jail, if Bethany had been stronger. She puts the image in a text and sends it to him, then deletes it from her phone, deletes him from her contacts too.

Finally, she finds and deletes the pictures she took of herself more than two years ago, the ones with the black eyes, the cut cheek and split lip. Electronic pigments of carmine and indigo and cuttlefish ink. The ones with the vivid bruising all up her side, thigh and hip and body; where it would turn out, when she finally saw a nurse months later, he'd fractured two of her ribs. Pictures taken with the abstract idea of using them as evidence, but she never showed anyone, just hid in her room in the dark, missing lectures and not answering her phone. Sitting in the library now, not looking at what might be around her, watching her, she waits a minute for a reply that she can also delete unread; but nothing happens. She rises to leave.

On the way out she does see the creepy bald man again after all. He's talking on his mobile while unchaining his bicycle. His bald skull-like head is now topped by a cycle helmet of neon green, but he's wearing his black hoodie. He's saying, 'Yeah but I *told* you this would happen. And now you're all like, oh my God. But I *warned* you, I really did. Why don't you ever *listen* to me? Puppies chew things, *deal* with it.' He glances once in Bethany's direction, not seeing her, before kicking off from the pavement and riding into the city's rush-hour traffic.

It's a week later when an old friend from undergraduate days, knowing a bit about Bethany's problems with the former professor, phones to tell her that he's dead.

'How?' Bethany asks, and even in the space of that word she imagines a dozen grotesque possibilities. Like, was he crucified upside down and disembowelled like that mysterious martyr in the illuminated gospel? Was he beheaded, tortured, boiled alive, flayed? Did a basilisk's gaze turn him to stone, shatter him into a thousand pieces? Or did one of those fucking creatures just eat him?

Luckily she doesn't voice any of this. Her friend tells her it was an accident. Well, and hypothermia, exposure, whatever. He slipped on the ice on his back patio, hit his head on a plant pot, knocked himself unconscious. It had just begun to snow, and the snow fell all night and covered his body. He froze to death. Any of a dozen neighbours might have seen him, a lump under the snow, and not known what it was. He had his mobile in his hand; its battery was dead, he'd been there so long. Bethany sees a square of snow illuminated by the phone's screen, dimming and dying. Days, they think. It was only as the thaw came that they found his body. Right there in his own back garden.

'God,' says Bethany.

'I would've thought the wife would've got the house, wouldn't you?' says her friend. 'Or maybe she didn't want anything associated with him, after ... well, you know.'

'Yes.'

'What're you feeling, Bethany? Talk to me.'

After they've hung up, Bethany cries. She hadn't really thought anything would happen. Hadn't really wondered whether she wanted anything to happen. Not that she's sorry. She'd not really meant to set the library's demons on this man who she once thought she'd loved, the man who hurt her so, who broke her life it seemed at the time for ever. Eventually, rumour and her teary breakdown before a faculty board had cost him his job, but nothing more. Until now.

She opens a bottle of wine almost automatically, pours herself a big glass — but then dumps it down the sink. Her boyfriend's still at work. It's dark, beginning to snow. She called her boyfriend the other night and he came running; can she call him to make him stay away? She knows now that it's safe to go back to the library. Knows that in fact it never meant her harm. Didn't even mean to scare her. All it wanted was to embrace her. And it has done. She will accept its gifts. It's where she'll go when she dies. Where she belongs. Forever. As if each stone were veined with her blood.

What better way to conclude our third volume of ghost stories than with a third appearance by Amanda Mason? Her first Fiction Desk contribution, 'No Good Deed', appeared in New Ghost Stories; *then* New Ghost Stories II *opened with her story 'Incomers'. Now, as she's the last one to leave, we must ask her to please turn out the lights...*

When the Dark Comes Down

Amanda Mason

'Will it be soon, do you think?' Rosie asked, sitting up.

'Soon enough.' The midwife, a round red-faced woman, was being no help at all. She was already at the sink, scrubbing her hands, her mind on her next patient.

Rosie debated repeating the question as she pulled up her thick woollen tights and zipped her boots, but she didn't quite have the nerve. She put on her coat, then wound her favourite scarf — the one her mum had made — around her neck. For a second or two it seemed that she could smell her mother's scent as she tugged it into place: lavender and lily of the valley.

Tears welled up in her eyes.

'Are you alright?' The expression on the other woman's face wasn't unkind, exactly. But her brisk manner — that morning's appointments were running late — didn't exactly invite confidences either. Twice now she had commented on the absence of a wedding ring, on the non-appearance of the baby's father. Rosie had tried to explain, but she wasn't certain the midwife had taken it in.

'I'm okay. A bit tired.' She pulled her mittens out of her pocket: she couldn't stand to look at her bare hands any longer.

'You're managing then, with the power cuts and everything?'

It was all anybody talked about these days, the cuts and the cold and the bloody miners.

'Yes. I — It's not much fun, is it?'

That wasn't what she'd meant to say, that wasn't it at all.

'Well, not long now,' said the midwife, turning back to her desk. 'You're doing very well.'

Rosie still hadn't got used to the weight of the baby she was carrying. Her back and breasts ached, and she walked slowly. She hadn't bloomed as her pregnancy progressed; as the weeks had gone by she had become sluggish, bloated, and bad tempered. She felt clumsy and foolish as she tried to negotiate the waiting room, her handbag bumping off people's knees and the two carrier bags of shopping she'd picked up on the way to the hospital swaying and threatening to split.

'Here you go, love,' one of the women stood and held the door open for her, smiling.

'Thanks.' She tried to smile back, ducking quickly through the door before the woman or anyone else could ask her when she was due and what she wanted, a boy or a girl. One day someone would ask her that — because once you were bloody pregnant, once you were showing, your body became everybody's business — and they wouldn't like her answer. They wouldn't like it one little bit.

The first thing she did when she got home was fill the kettle and set it to boil on the hob, grateful once again for the reliable whoosh of the gas, the solid blue flame. She checked her watch and switched the radio on; she'd catch the news and maybe put her feet up for a while. She had plenty to do — the cot she'd bought second-hand needed assembling for one thing — but the walk back from the hospital through the slushy streets, followed by the climb up thirty-seven worn and uneven steps to the cottage at the top of White Horse Yard, had defeated her yet again.

She was fed up of that too. The way she'd woken first thing in the morning, filled once more with good intentions, only to have her body — invaded by this person she was suddenly entirely responsible for — conspire against her once again. She hadn't always felt like this. It had come on her slowly, as her pregnancy had gone on, as they'd started work on the house, as the strike had begun and they'd had to get used to the cold and the dark.

The kettle was whistling and she'd missed the news headlines. As if things were going to be different anyway. She made herself a cup of tea, padding carefully around on her stockinged feet, a little self-conscious, the tiny kitchen with its old pine table and its brand new oven, all of it still a little unfamiliar.

The news bulletin ended and a man started singing. She liked this one. It made her think of Dan, of slow dancing in the dark, soft kisses, and his arms around her.

'Home,' she said softly, as she sat at the table and reached for the packet of ginger biscuits.

Home.

The house had been built in 1772, which made it exactly two hundred years old. When they'd first come to look around, Dan had fallen in love.

The place needed a bit of work, he'd told her, but underneath the years of use and amateur improvements it was perfect. Perfect. His mum, Penny, had accompanied them on their second visit and she'd been less impressed.

'Why don't you buy something modern, something new?' she'd asked, before pointing out yet again that they were building a new estate up by the park, not so very far away from her own house.

Rosie had taken Dan's side almost as a matter of principle, not bothering after that to show him the ads featuring bigger, lighter houses that wouldn't require any DIY, that might better suit a young couple just starting out, that Penny might approve of. So here she was, sitting with her cup of tea in her little cottage with its sash windows and low ceilings and poky rooms.

She — they — had been there for almost five months now, with Dan doing a little more every time he got home. Stripping the woodwork, tearing away the wallpaper upstairs, pulling out the modern panelling and exposing the original walls downstairs; every trip home revealing a little more of the house, as it used to be.

She had helped him at first. She'd always enjoyed working with her hands, but as she'd grown heavier she'd done less, and as more of the cottage had been revealed her enthusiasm had cooled. She wasn't sure why — it was something do to with the damp bare stone and the plain wood they had revealed, something to do with the small windows and the dim light and the cramped cold feeling she got sometimes.

She tried not to think about it too much.

She let her hands rest gently on her belly and closed her eyes.

'He'll be home soon,' she said, softly.

The cot lay in flat pieces stacked against the bedroom wall. It had been a bargain, and it would have been foolish to turn it down, despite Dan's mumbled misgivings and his mother's insistence that she'd be happy to buy them a nice new one from Mothercare. It was a bit old, but perfectly serviceable.

It had been Jeannie Eglon who had offered the cot, catching Rosie on her own one day as she was going out to do some shopping. Nipping out of her front door which opened straight into the yard — she must have been keeping a careful eye out — and making the offer with no preamble. When she'd bought it, Rosie had a vague idea of stripping it down and varnishing it; the kind of idea her previous not-pregnant self might have had, the girl who had the energy to help Dan strip the wallpaper in the spare bedroom, the girl who didn't want to get married, didn't want to be tied down.

Now she realised that the best she could hope for would be to put it together without incident and to give it a good clean. She could live with the peeling paint on the legs and the large and cheerful kittens in pink silky bows printed on the headboard. After all, the baby wouldn't care.

'There's plenty of use in it yet,' Jeannie Eglon had said the day she brought it round, once the two of them had manhandled the last pieces upstairs. She'd sat on the bed, fanning herself and trying not to look as though she was inspecting everything.

'Yes.'

'You have been busy, haven't you?' Jeannie was bouncing gently up and down, as if she might swing her legs up, lean back and take forty winks. She wasn't really that much older than Rosie, not when you stopped to think about it, for all that she had five children. She was probably not quite into her thirties: she'd started young, that was all.

'I suppose so.'

'It'll be lovely when you're done.'

'I — thanks.'

'Will Danny be back in time?'

'Time?'

'For, you know.' Jeannie nodded towards the bulge underneath Rosie's smock.

'Oh. Yes. I suppose so.'

'Good money. On the rigs.'

'Yes.'

Five children. Rosie couldn't imagine it. She could barely imagine one.

'I couldn't just use your loo, could I?'

'Oh. Yes. Of course —'

'Ma-aa-am...' A child's fretful voice echoed up the stairs, 'Maa-aam... Where are you?'

'Oh, God.' Jeannie shot to her feet, 'I could have sworn I shut the door.'

Rosie followed her down the stairs to the hall where one of the middle children, Marion or Marianne, stood, her nose running and her hair tousled. As soon as she saw her mother she burst into tears.

'What did I tell you?' Jeannie demanded. Without bothering to wait for an answer she dragged the child, who should surely have been in school, out of the front door.

'Thank you for the cot,' Rosie had called from the front step.

Jeannie hadn't looked back.

It was simple enough to put together in the end. All she lacked was a new mattress, and that would have to wait until Dan's mum next came to visit. She left the old one propped up against the bedroom wall. Like the cot, it had seen better days and smelt of Dettol and stale milk. She would put it in the spare room later — the baby's room — and get Dan to take it to the tip. The cot still needed a clean though. She sat down on the bed, trying to ease her aching back.

She woke in a panic. In the dark. Not sure where she was or what day it was. *The power,* was her first half-formed thought; *candles,* the second. She'd forgotten to light a candle.

She hauled herself to her feet, blinking furiously, the bedroom coming into gradual focus. The light outside had faded, but she could still see well enough. When she checked her watch, she realised it wasn't yet five and that she still had a little more time before they cut off the electricity.

Panic was replaced by relief: all she had to do was flick a switch on the wall. She thought she had done that already when she entered the room. She could have sworn she had: it was second nature by now in this house — she pushed the thought away.

More confident now that she knew the dark was not a permanent condition, she made her way to the door and switched on the light.

The cot was where she'd left it, wedged between the wardrobe and the wall, but it was no good in the corner there. Dan's mum was of the opinion the baby should start off in his own room but neither Rosie nor Dan were happy with that. They'd have to think about rearranging the furniture when he got back.

She remembered to check the dressing table to make sure there were candles and the saucers to stand them in; the few candlesticks they owned were downstairs in the living room. There were two boxes of matches: one for the bedside table, the other for the tall chest of drawers. She unplugged the bedside light and put it on the floor, replacing it with the large and unlovely oil lamp Penny had delivered a couple of weeks ago.

When she was done, she surveyed the room and was tempted to sit back down on the bed and ease the throbbing in her back for a moment or two. She glanced out of the window at the dark blue sky. She could light a candle and leave it burning. Just in case she fell asleep. But she daren't. Dan wouldn't like it.

'You have to promise,' he had insisted.

'Dan.'

'Promise.'

No leaving a flame unattended, no falling asleep with a candle still burning. The stories you heard these days. A little lass scarred for life, a woman killed in a house fire. She'd never seen Dan so serious before. And no wandering about the house with a naked flame, he'd said; she had to agree to use a torch when she needed to go up and downstairs.

'I promise,' she'd said.

She'd never thought about it before, never properly realised how much they all relied on the electricity just being there, all the time, waiting to be used. That it wasn't anymore, not always, bothered her. It wasn't so easy to chase the dark away with a thin candle that flickered and sent shadows dancing up the walls and across the ceiling. Not in this house.

She smoothed down the covers on the bed, resisting the temptation to check her watch again: she didn't want to think about the time, about time running out.

She made her way downstairs, wondering again if she might not be better off sleeping in the living room to save herself the effort of the staircase. It was getting harder and harder to manage; she was beginning to dread going up and downstairs with a baby in her arms. As usual, she abandoned the idea. At least the loo was upstairs.

She ate slowly; the radio, spare batteries close by, playing softly in the background. She washed up in front of the kitchen window with only her reflection, bloated and unrecognisable, for company.

Dan rang just as she was putting everything away. A single plate, a cup, and a saucepan. A wooden spoon and a knife and fork. She waddled towards the phone – smart shiny red plastic – that they kept on the little table by the front door.

'Hello?' She couldn't help sounding unsure every time she answered, even though it was unlikely to be anyone else. 'Dan?'

'Hello, beautiful.'

She wanted to cry. It wasn't fair, the way his voice would do that to her – make her fall for him all over again.

'Dan?'

'Well, who else? The milkman?'

She leant back against the wall. 'Dan,' she said again. The light was dim in the hall; the candles in the kitchen gave out a pale, helpless sort of glow.

'Are you alright, love?'

'Fine. Yes. I'm fine.'

'And my little lad?'

He had insisted it was a boy they were expecting; he had done from the moment she'd told him.

'Kicking.' Right on cue, the baby shifted and Rosie placed a hand on the spot where she imagined his foot was flexing. 'When can you come home?'

Dan was on the rigs two weeks on and two weeks off, and Jeannie Eglon was right, the money was good, but Rosie was beginning to wonder if that made up for the way she missed him these days. She'd always thought of herself as independent, happy in her own company, but since falling pregnant she'd begun to fret as the days and nights Dan spent away stretched out in front of her.

'Next week, just like we said. Unless there's a – you know – an emergency. Why? Are you not well?'

'I'm okay. I just – miss you.'

'And I miss you.' He'd lowered his voice though, so as not to be overheard, 'There's always Mum. If you get worried or anything.'

'I know.'

'Have you seen her recently?'

'Not for a few days.' There was no point in lying: he'd be ringing her later anyway, if he hadn't already. And she had seen Penny briefly, at the beginning of the week. She had been round to deliver a set of Babygros — lemon and white, impossibly small and clean — and had stayed for a cup of tea. Officially, she had no objection to Rosie and Dan not being married, to her first grandchild being born out of wedlock. But she wasn't exactly pleased either. 'She wants me to go round for tea on Sunday.' The better to discuss baby names, no doubt.

'She means well,' Dan was saying.

'Yes,' said Rosie, 'I know.'

She was back in the kitchen, sweeping the floor, when the power went off. Seven o'clock, on the dot.

It was tempting to stay where she was: she could light the oven again for warmth and she had the radio; but her back was aching again and part of her, the sensible part, knew that it was foolish to put off the moment when she'd have to extinguish the candles and go into the darkened living room. She looked around the kitchen, making sure that it was tidy, that she hadn't left the gas on. She wiped down the counter tops and the handles of the cupboards; she cleaned the sink and draped a dishcloth over the taps.

There.

All done.

She wasn't sure, but she may have spoken aloud.

It was too early to go to bed.

She wished they'd managed to get rid of the electric fire in the front room. For all the work it involved, the clearing out of ashes, the bother of filling a coal scuttle and fetching it in, she missed the crackling living warmth of a coal fire. Never mind the times the wind gusted down the chimney and smoke billowed through the room.

They'd get around to it one day, she supposed. One day, when things got back to normal and they could rely on the coal and the power again.

She blew out the candles one by one, then stood in the doorway, holding the last candle in its saucer, making sure there was nothing she'd overlooked. The flame wavered a little and it seemed for a moment that the dark was moving closer, wrapping itself around her.

'Stupid.'

It was an old house, that was all.

She left the kitchen, resolutely not looking back, and opened the living room door. She'd left the candles in place that morning, and spare boxes of matches on the mantelpiece and the coffee table. A second oil lamp graciously donated by Penny, bigger and uglier than the one upstairs, stood on the sideboard underneath the window.

Humming softly under her breath — a quiet, monotonous scrap of something she'd heard on the radio — she went around the room lighting candles, not hurrying. Not exactly hurrying anyway, and only closing the door once she was ready to tackle the paraffin heater. They'd bought it when the strike first started; it was a large ugly metal box set on casters, and was just like the one her mum used to have when Rosie was a kid. It was better than nothing, she supposed.

By the time she was done — the door closed, the fire lit, the book to hand — she was oddly flustered and slightly out of breath.

It was the same every evening, as soon as the electricity went off. Daft, really.

'You're managing,' the midwife had asked, 'with the power cuts and everything?'

Not exactly, she should have said. Not really.

She hadn't been like this before; nervous and easily startled, scared of her own shadow. She couldn't quite work out if it was because of the baby, or the house, or the strike. She wondered sometimes if it was the dark, the way it seemed to fit into the little cottage, to fill it in a way she and Dan never would.

She squashed this thought as she picked up her book: the house was just stone and tiles and wood. It was their home now, and they were going to be happy here.

She read for an hour or so, managing to lose herself for a little while until the pressure on her bladder became more than she could ignore. She put her book down and picked up the torch she'd left on the table. She pushed at the switch: nothing.

She sat forward and gave the torch a shake and was rewarded with a faint yellow beam which flickered for a moment or two before fading away.

'Shit.'

She picked up a candle set on a little blue saucer and made her way back into the kitchen. The batteries by the radio were the wrong size; that much was obvious straight away. She looked in the kitchen drawer where she could have sworn she'd put a spare set but there was nothing there. She opened a couple of cupboards, uncomfortably aware that the urge to pee was getting stronger by the moment.

'Fine.'

She'd look later.

She went back into the hall.

They hadn't got round to doing much with the staircase yet. It was a bit of a bodge job, Dan had announced, what with the way it seemed to have been pushed in behind the living room as some sort of afterthought. It was thickly carpeted, and the way it turned steeply in and around on itself always made Rosie think of the spiral stairs inside a lighthouse. There was no handrail to speak of, although some previous owner had rigged up a rope substitute, attaching it to the wooden wall panels with large dull brass rings. They had thought it nautical, perhaps, and probably hadn't minded the way the rope had become slightly greasy through wear.

It always seemed worse in the dark.

It wasn't so very bad until she reached the first turn, which cut off the distant comforting glow of the living room and where, she could almost swear, the staircase narrowed as it folded around on itself, the walls pressing in. This was the point where she was always tempted to abandon decorum and scramble the rest of the way using her hands as well as her feet — well, where she had always been tempted before. To double over like that now would be beyond her. She took a steadying breath or two and focused on the dancing golden flame she held, the way it shimmered at her slightest movement, the way she seemed to pull it along in her wake as she made her careful way up the stairs.

When she got to the bathroom, she placed the candle on the corner of the bath and struggled onto the loo, wondering about going into the bedroom now she was up here, lighting a candle or two, maybe getting ready for bed. She counted the days she had left: the days until she'd see Dan again, the days until her due date.

It was cold at the top of the house and she shivered as she pulled up her tights and washed her hands and —

Her skirt must have brushed against the saucer as she reached for the towel. It tilted slowly and slid down into the bath in a lazy circling sweep, losing the candle which rolled and guttered, then expired.

She was alone.

In the dark.

Close your eyes. Hadn't her mum always told her that? Close your eyes when you switch out the light, and then when you open them you'll be able to see. She couldn't. She couldn't do that.

Was there a moon tonight? Maybe there was moonlight. She turned her head to where she knew the window was: the frosted glass was too thick to let any light through.

The bedroom, then. Candles there, and matches too. How many steps across the little carpeted landing? Four? Five? She turned herself around, leaning against the sink. She was facing the door now, and beyond, just a few steps away — a half dozen, no more than that — lay her bedroom and an oil lamp and a window and a moonlit starry night.

If only she could move.

She had to force herself to take the first tentative step, arms stretched out, her right hand brushing past the useless light cord, her knuckles catching painfully against the door jamb as she found the door handle and stepped out of the little bathroom. To her right was the staircase; ahead, more or less, the bedroom. She hesitated.

One more step, two. The bedroom door seemed to rise up, connecting painfully with foot, knee, and hand all at once.

'Shit!'

The door swung back, and she stepped in.

It wasn't so bad here. To her left she could make out the bedside table. She stretched out both hands again and edged forward, her fingertips finding the top of the cabinet, running over the familiar things she'd left there: hairbrush; book; the base of the lamp, cool and reassuring.

Matches, matches, matches.

She couldn't find them.

She started over, trying to be methodical, working left to right.

She brushed against them, the corner of the cardboard box catching briefly under her nails then vanishing; she grabbed at them, but there was nothing there.

The window, then. She'd open the curtains, and that would help. Even if she'd misplaced this matchbox, knocked it to the floor in her panic, then there was another on the dressing table. She straightened up. The shadows here were familiar, and at least without a light flickering they stayed where they should.

The baby's cot caught her on the hip as she was negotiating the foot of the bed. She swore again and tried to ignore the terrible urge she had to cry.

God almighty, Rosie. Just get to the curtains and pull them back.

She squeezed between the cot and the bed, inching forward carefully, as if the floor might fall away from underneath her feet. She was almost at the window when something grabbed at her, pushing at her arm and shoulder — she pushed back hard, too hard, and lost her balance, tumbling across the foot of the bed and onto the floor, landing clumsily on her hands and knees. Her assailant gave way and fell with her, soft and silent.

Dettol and stale milk.

The mattress, the stupid bloody mattress.

She'd forgotten it was there.

She almost laughed.

The mattress, that's all.

She pulled herself slowly to her feet and made her way to the window.

She opened the curtains and let her head rest against the chilled glass. She couldn't see the moon, or many stars come to that, but she could see the steps down from her front door to the yard; she could see her neighbours' houses again, and the dull orange lights that flickered in their windows.

It's dark in there too.

She smoothed her jumper down over her belly. 'It's alright,' she said, as if saying it out loud would make it so.

She looked at her watch, but couldn't quite make out the time. Rubbing absently at her hip, she turned away from the window. She could make out the room a little more clearly now: the familiar bulge of the bed, the wardrobe, the dressing table. The mattress sprawled on the floor, the little cot in the corner.

Maybe she should have put it in the spare room after all; maybe Penny was right about starting as they meant to go on.

The candles were where she'd left them on the dressing table, and she could make out the saucers too, but the matches... She leant closer and gently ran her fingers over the table: a pair of earrings, discarded tissues, bits of makeup, and the wooden jewellery box her grandfather had given her when she was a little girl.

No matches.

No. Try again. Left to right again and moving carefully, resisting the temptation to pick things up, all the useless bits of rubbish she kept there, and throw them onto the floor until she found –

She had the strangest sensation there was someone there, behind her in the room, in the dark, waiting.

'No.'

She stood up and turned around and the room was still. Everything was where it should be, everything in its place.

No.

She ran her hand over her belly again.

She'd try one more time, then give up and fetch a light from downstairs. She turned her back on the room, the hairs on her neck prickling, her heart thudding, her hip and belly aching.

The matches were there on the table where she'd left them, next to the saucers. The first match flared and died, and she fumbled with the second, almost dropping it before managing to light her candle.

She raised her arm; the pale golden light shivered in front of her, and beyond it the shadows deepened. And still there was that sensation, that she was no longer alone.

What if there's someone in the house?

She'd read the stories in the papers, everyone had. People being broken into, robbed, worse. But she'd locked the door that afternoon, she was certain of it. And anyway, in the dark, wouldn't an intruder struggle as much as she?

What if there's something in the dark?

She wouldn't think about that. That was ... stupid.

She wondered about lighting the other candles, but she didn't trust the trembling in her fingers. Besides, she was going to go downstairs now and she'd be sleeping on the sofa tonight and peeing in a saucepan if she had to, because she wasn't coming back up here in the dark, not for anything. Tomorrow she'd take that bloody cot apart and get it shifted and be rid of the bloody mattress and —

She tried to catch her breath. To think.

She could hardly scramble one-handed across the bed. She'd have to make her way between it and the cot again, but that would be alright, because she had her candle now.

She stepped forward, the candle in her left hand, wax dribbling down the pillar onto her fingers where it cooled and hardened, the little box of matches gripped firmly in her right: she didn't entirely trust them not to vanish again if she let them go.

She walked as quickly as she dared towards the stairs, one hand raised, the other still clutching the box of matches, trying at the same time to guard the flame as it danced and jerked in the dark. She was at the top of the staircase when she felt it again: the strange and distinct sensation that there was someone or something behind her in the dark. She turned, raising the candle up too suddenly, too swiftly. The flame flattened, spluttered, and vanished, and the dark settled round her again.

What if there's –

'No.' She tried to force it away, that panicky, prickling sensation that seemed to dance over her skin. 'No,' she said, louder this time, listening for a moment or two for an answer.

Gingerly she turned and lowered herself onto the first stair, lay the candle in her lap, and opened the box of matches. The first one she struck snapped, and as she opened the box again she spilled a handful onto the carpet. She leant forward, hoping to rescue one or two as a sharp cold draft played against the back of her neck.

'No.' She forced herself to be still, took in a breath and then exhaled. The next match caught and flared and she reached for the candle, but it had gone.

'Shit.' She ran her fingers over the thick pile of the carpet again: the candle must have rolled away as she'd been trying to retrieve the matches.

Standing and walking back up the little hallway seemed impossible. Going back to the bedroom was out of the question. That she might pick up a second candle there seemed poor compensation for turning away from the stairs and risking the dark again, and anyway she'd been away from the living room for too long; away from all those candles, warm and bright, burning away unattended.

The stories you heard.

She struck another match and looked down the stairs. Safer to bump herself down on her bum, perhaps, one step at a time. Easier, even, without the candle to worry about. The match she held flared, and she held it for as long as she dared before the heat reached her fingers, before the charred tip turned up on itself and crumpled away. She blew it out at the last possible moment, frowning as bright orange sparks fell onto the carpet and died.

We're going to do this, she thought, me and you, kid.

Now.

She slid herself forward, one step, two, three. She held the box of matches firmly in her left hand, kicked forward with her slippered feet, and lowered herself inelegantly onto the stairs.

She'd laugh about this once it was over, and the next time she spoke to Dan on the phone, she'd make him laugh too — she'd save it up and make it into a comedy of errors for him. *I had to come down on my arse in the end, you should have seen me.* She imagined him sitting across the table from her rather than at the far end of a telephone line. Shaking his head, laughing at her.

Kicking out, she made contact with the wall.

'Fuck.'

She stretched out her right hand; above her head the rope looped along the wall, cold and slightly damp.

Nearly there.

She kicked out more cautiously, but still managed to misjudge it, losing control and lurching forward, the base of her spine thudding painfully down the next couple of stairs.

It wasn't funny. It wasn't funny at all and tears sprang into her eyes. She was tired, so very tired of it all: Dan's mum and the power cuts and the dark and the cold and the way her body was no longer her own and the way everyone thought they owned a piece of her now, the way they would smile and pat her belly and tell her their own little horror stories. She was frightened too, because the world had never seemed so terrifying before and here she was barely able to manage the stairs and her back was hurting — her hip too, where she'd bashed it earlier. And how was she ever going to manage any of this alone, any of it?

Christ.

She stopped to think; to consider the nature of the pain, the dull ache that seemed to be building inside her.

No.

Not that.

Not now.

She righted herself and decided to risk another match, fumbling for a moment before carefully picking one out, striking it and lifting it up to eye level. She was, she reckoned, about halfway down the stairs — the ache in her back had subsided and after all, she was almost there.

The dark behind her shifted and another cold breeze ran across her neck before reaching the little gold flame she held; it bent double for a moment, almost righted itself but then gave up, sighing. She was left in the dark again.

No.

She kicked out again, kicked and slid, kicked and slid, her skirt catching and rising up as she went, her hands slipping on the unwieldy carpet until she kicked back the curtain at the bottom of the stairs and sat stock still.

The hall stretched out in front of her, entirely dark.

There should have been light. She'd left the door open, letting the candles cast a comforting pale pool into the hall, and she was afraid for a moment that she'd been away too long, that they had all burned themselves out; that the darkness had overtaken her during her struggle downstairs.

The door was closed, that was all. That this didn't make sense wasn't something she could think about right now. All she had to do was push herself to her feet and —

She felt it again: a silent billowing of the air.

No.

She scrambled to her feet, breathless, the bruise on her hip pulling again — the stupid cot, she should have waited for Dan to help her put it together. She reached out and placed one hand against the wall, the wallpaper they'd chosen together smooth and cool under her fingers.

She'd never wanted to live in an old house: you were never properly alone. She'd tried to tell Dan that once, but hadn't been able to find the words.

She pushed the door open, and there was the living room, warm, safe, just as she'd left it, the lamp and the candles promising protection. She'd be fine now. There was light enough to last until dawn, and then she'd go to Penny's and ask to stay and only come back here once Dan was home.

She was still standing in the doorway as the pain struck again, the pulling sensation slicing through her. She gasped and leant against the wall, struggling to catch her breath.

What if there was no one there?

She took one step forward, two.

What if —

One of the candles on the coffee table flickered and died. Its twin followed suit, as did the fat candle she'd set in the centre of the table in an old glass dish. Thin tapers in their brass candlesticks on the mantelpiece were snuffed out, one by one, smoke curling up into the fading light. The lamp in the corner with its green glass bell seemed to tremble and its glow began to fade and finally there was only a single candle on the sideboard to hold the dark at bay.

What if there was nothing there?

She was still clutching the box of matches, which split in her grip as she staggered and fell forward onto her knees once more.

She would wait; wait for this to pass and then get up, get to the phone, get to the front door, get out, get away. As soon as she got her breath back, as soon as —

What if it was just the dark?

'No.'

It was a live, liquid thing, filling the room.

No.

She saw the last candle tremble and fall, rolling off the old saucer, off the sideboard and onto the rag rug. Its flame flattened and pooled against the fabric for a long moment. If it caught, she wasn't sure she could get up and get away. The rug was old. It would burn bright and fierce, she was sure it would. It would spread to the carpets, the sofa, the curtains. She curved one arm around her stomach and waited, helpless.

The stories you heard.

The flame struggled up, jerked briefly, then fell back defeated.

She closed her eyes.

She couldn't move.

She was alone in the dark.

And it knew she was there.

About the Contributors

Richard Agemo lives in Washington, DC. He writes historical fiction and blogs about Shakespeare. His forthcoming novel is about a sixteenth century poet who's framed for treason.

Will Dunn is a journalist from London. Alongside classic ghost stories by the likes of Algernon Blackwood, he enjoys short science fiction, from HG Wells to John Wyndham to Kurt Vonnegut, as well as the short fiction of Raymond Carver, Alice Munro and John Cheever. Will works at the *New Statesman* and writes fiction in his spare time. He is currently finishing work on his first novel.

Philippa East originally studied psychology and philosophy at university and in her day job she works as a clinical psychologist. Her prize-winning stories have been published in various magazines including *Brittle Star*, *Fictive Dream*, *The Lampeter Review* and *For Books' Sake*. Originally from Scotland, Philippa now lives in Lincolnshire where she is currently completing her first novel, under the mentorship of Judith Allnat.

Jerry Ibbotson has been a BBC journalist, has worked in the games industry and been a writer for hire. He has self-published two urban fantasy novels and recently started an MA in creative writing. He currently works in a convent. He lives in York, where there are tales of ghosts and gore around every corner.

Seth Marlin is an internationally published writer, activist, educator, and slam performer. He holds an MFA in Creative Writing from Eastern Washington University, and is the author of *Shred*, a chapbook of poetry. His stories and verse have appeared in *Spark*, *Knockout*, *A cappella Zoo*, and *Silk Road Review*, among others. He resides in the American Pacific Northwest.

Amanda Mason is a graduate of Dartington College of Arts, where she studied theatre and began writing by devising and directing her own plays. After a few years of earning a very irregular living in lots of odd jobs, including performing in a comedy street magic act, she became a teacher and has worked in the UK, Italy, Spain, and Germany.

She now lives in York and has given up teaching for writing. Her short stories have been included in various anthologies including The Fiction Desk's *New Ghost Stories* and *New Ghost Stories II*.

Barney Walsh lives in the north of England, where he completed his MA in creative writing at the University of Manchester. His stories have appeared in journals and anthologies including *The Warwick Review*, *Unthology* 4 and 7, *Litro Magazine*, *Shooter Literary Magazine*, *The Manchester Review*, *The Honest Ulsterman*, and *Cōnfingō*. He was shortlisted for the 2016 Royal Academy and Pin Drop Short Story Award. Sometimes there are tweets: @BarneyEWalsh.

For more information on the contributors
to this volume, please visit our website:

www.thefictiondesk.com/authors

Also Available

www.thefictiondesk.com